She kept her face averted while he tried to see it in the shadow.

At last he said, 'You're all wrought up. I'm sorry if it's so traumatic for you. . . .' He paused, then added, 'I'll be leaving early in the morning, but I'll be back just as soon as I can. . . . I promise. We'll talk then. Okay?'

She didn't answer or give him any sign.

He let out a long, exasperated breath and forced her mouth to meet his. His kiss was long and hard and angry. When it was over he sighed again and pushed her inside. 'Remember, I'll be back.'

LAUREY BRIGHT

has held a number of different jobs, but she has never wanted to be anything but a writer. She lives in New Zealand, where she creates the stories of contemporary people in love that have won her a following all over the world.

Dear Reader,

Silhouette Special Editions are an exciting new line of contemporary romances from Silhouette Books. Special Editions are written specifically for our readers who want a story with heightened romantic tension.

Special Editions have all the elements you've enjoyed in Silhouette Romances and *more*. These stories concentrate on romance in a longer, more realistic and sophisticated way, and they feature greater sensual detail.

I hope you enjoy this book and all the wonderful romances from Silhouette.

Karen Solem
Editor-in-Chief
Silhouette Books

LAUREY BRIGHT
When Morning Comes

Silhouette Special Edition

Published by Silhouette Books New York

America's Publisher of Contemporary Romance

Silhouette Books by Laurey Bright

Tears of Morning (Rom #107)
Sweet Vengeance (Rom #125)
Deep Waters (SE #62)
When Morning Comes (SE #143)

SILHOUETTE BOOKS, a Division of Simon & Schuster, Inc.
1230 Avenue of the Americas, New York, N.Y. 10020

ISBN: 0-671-53643-5

First Silhouette Books printing January, 1984

10 9 8 7 6 5 4 3 2 1

Map by Ray Lundgren

SILHOUETTE, SILHOUETTE SPECIAL EDITION and
colophon are registered trademarks of Simon & Schuster, Inc.

America's Publisher of Contemporary Romance

Printed in the U.S.A.

When Morning Comes

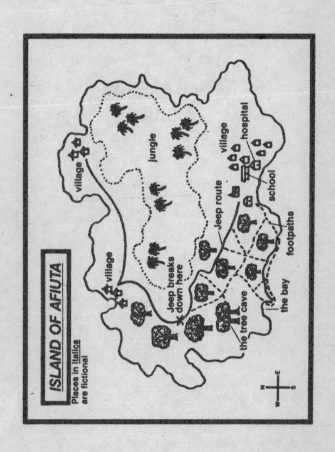

Chapter One

Claire saw the sail outside the reef just before the yacht came about and began to dance effortlessly through the narrow channel to the lagoon. It wasn't that easy, she knew; whoever captained the vessel had to be a skilled sailor to make it look so simple, guiding his craft between the sharp coral outcrops into safe water. But he wasn't one of the locals. This was not a native outrigger canoe with a triangle of coconut-matting sail, or a trading schooner, slow and shabby, coming to collect the copra, the island's only export, and sell tinned goods, lengths of cotton and kitchen utensils in exchange. Even at a distance its white canvas was dazzling, its dark orange paintwork pristine, and its sharply graceful lines proclaimed speed, style—and luxury.

Unease started right then, at her first sight of the

Bella Donna. In the ten months she had been on the island, the only visitors had been traders, and natives from nearby atolls. This was an alien, the kind of vessel that belonged in the tourist havens of Papeete and Vila, not in the quiet lagoon waters of Afiuta, named for its 'fine shore,' but only a small, almost forgotten atoll in the Polynesian fringe of the Solomons.

The children had seen the yacht, too. Their small brown faces were alight with curiosity, and one by one they jumped up from the woven pandanus mats they had been sitting on and began chattering excitedly in a mixture of pidgin and their local dialect. The school had no walls, only a thatched roof and stout poles supporting it to which Claire had nailed a chalkboard and some boards to hold charts and pictures. There were woven mats rolled up around the sides which could be pulled down when it rained, but on fine days it was cooler to leave it open.

She knew that there was no chance of further lessons that day. The advent of the strange yacht was too novel an event for her to hope to hold their interest. In any case, it was almost time for dismissal, so she yielded to their pleas and let them scamper through the coconut palms and down to the beach on bare brown feet. They ran along the shore, whooping and shouting and calling out questions and comments to each other and even to the unseen occupants of the yacht which was slowly coming closer, but was still too distant to allow them to be heard. Some children splashed into the water, apparently intending to swim out to meet the visitors, while their companions fell about laughing at their ambition, and Claire looked on a little anxiously until the intrepid ones realised that the yacht was too far away and returned to the shore. The island children swam like fish almost from birth, and could probably have made it, but the lagoon was miles wide, and they would have been exhausted by the effort.

Claire glanced at the low white buildings housing the mission hospital with its kitchen annexe and living quarters for the staff. No one came onto the wide veranda, and she guessed that Sister Amy and Sister Loretta were too busy with their patients to notice the sail out in the lagoon, and Sister Martha's kitchen domain faced inland. Father Damien was on the other side of the island visiting a sick old woman who had been unable to attend Mass the previous Sunday.

For a few minutes Claire remained watching the yacht until figures appeared on deck to furl the sails and an anchor chain was let go, rattling into the water. Something stronger than curiosity then sent her hurrying over to the hospital, her sandalled feet soundless on the sparse tough grass.

She looked back once at the yacht before plunging through the open doorway almost as though hiding from some pursuit. When her eyes adjusted to the interior light after the brilliance of the tropical sun, she saw Sister Amy coming towards her, her round brown face split by a wide, welcoming smile. Claire came every day after school finished at one o'clock to help out in the hospital outpatients' clinic and the kitchen where the evening meals for staff and patients were prepared, but every afternoon the native sister greeted her with the same friendly appreciation, as if she was doing the nursing staff a great

favour for which they never stopped being grateful.
It was heartwarming, and the sight of the familiar,
beaming smile steadied Claire's odd near-panic.

'You're early today,' Sister Amy said, making it
sound like a lovely surprise.

'There's a boat,' Claire told her quite calmly. 'A
yacht, just come into the lagoon. I let the children go
down to the beach to watch it anchor.'

'Visitors?' Sister Amy went to the door and
peeped out. 'I wonder who it is?'

Sister Amy was plump, with sturdy legs showing
below the hem of her calf-length white habit which
was really only a simple cotton frock with a front
zipper, and although her face was smooth and
ageless, there were wisps of grey in the frizz of black
hair that escaped from the short white veil she wore.
But as she looked out at the newcomer in the
tranquil lagoon, her dark eyes shining with interest,
for an instant Claire had a picture in her mind's eye
of Sister Amy as a child, scampering down to the
beach with the others. Then the nun turned and said,
'Well, I suppose we'll find out sooner or later. And
as you're here, maybe you could see that everything's made ready in the clinic, Claire.'

In the small, antiseptic room Claire set to work
with practised movements, setting out clean cloths
and stainless-steel basins, and removing instruments
from the old but still efficient steriliser to lay them
ready. She didn't know what some of them were for,
but two of the sisters were qualified nurses. The
doctor came only once a month, and in between
times they ran the clinic and hospital.

She checked the shelves of supplies, and added to
the list on the wall a couple of items that seemed to

be getting low. Then she tied a clean white cloth about her head, almost like the simple veils the nuns wore, and automatically straightened her white cotton shirtwaister frock and pinned one of the nurses' aprons over it. On the desk she placed the file drawer holding the cards with the names and medical histories of all their patients for the sister to refer to. There were only five hundred or so people on the entire island, and Sister Amy knew all of them and their ailments, but she was very strict about proper medical procedures being followed.

Sister Amy arrived about twenty minutes before the clinic was due to start, and shortly afterwards a forceful knock on the door made Claire glance up from the notes she had been taking under the nun's direction. A European face was there—no, two of them. One man supported the other as they came in, closing the door behind them with his free hand, and it was obvious which was the patient. He was flushed and sweating, and his right arm was encased in a quite professional-looking sling. His eyes were half-closed, and he almost fell onto the couch when Sister Amy, after one startled glance, motioned his companion to help him to it.

He moaned as he lay down, and the other man, tall and broad-shouldered, with sun-streaked light brown hair, muttered, 'Sorry, Eddie. We'll soon have you right.'

'What is his name, please?' Sister Amy asked briskly, bending over the sick man.

Claire drew a card towards her on the desk, pen poised. The tall fair man answered, 'Eddie Robson. He's a crewman on my yacht. He slipped and broke his arm a few days ago. . . . I set it, but some sort of infection seems to have got in. We were told by radio that there was a hospital here.'

Claire wrote down the details as he gave them. He had a pleasant voice, deep and attractively timbred, with a slight Australian accent that reminded her of home.

Sister Amy, gently removing the sling, asked, 'You have medical knowledge?'

'Very little. Nobody else on board has any.'

'I see.' She spoke quietly to the injured man, but he only grunted in reply and turned his head aside as though too tired to speak.

There was a silence, broken by the heavy breathing of the patient, while Sister Amy uncovered the wound. 'You have splinted it quite well,' she said, 'but you're right about the infection. I don't think that the bone will need resetting, but it's difficult to tell because the area is swollen.'

'Shouldn't a doctor see him?' the man asked.

'Probably,' Sister Amy answered equably. 'Unfortunately, we don't expect her for three weeks. You will have to trust Mr. Robson to us, Mr. . . . .'

'Carver—Scott Carver.' He paused. 'You *are* a nurse, aren't you? I mean—'

Sister Amy laughed. 'I was trained in Australia, Mr. Carver. Don't worry. I'm a fully qualified sister—in both senses of the word.'

'I apologise.'

'No, there's no need. I think Mr. Robson should stay in the hospital for a few days. We'll give him antibiotics and keep an eye on the arm. Will you be able to stay and wait for him to recover?'

'Yes. We're in no hurry.'

'Your boat isn't a racing yacht?'

'I have raced her, but at the moment I'm on a leisurely cruise with a group of friends.'

'That's nice.' Without turning, Sister Amy said, 'Claire, bring me a wide bandage, please.'

Claire brought it from the shelf in the corner, and Scott Carver moved aside to allow her to hand it to the nun. She felt his eyes appraising her and stepped back quickly to return to the desk.

The sick man moaned again and tried to pull away as Sister Amy carefully lifted his arm.

'I don't think he knows what he's doing half the time,' Scott Carver said. 'He's been delirious with pain and fever. . . . Shall I hold him?'

'We'll see. Claire,' the nun said, 'please go and take over in the ward for a little while, and ask Sister Loretta if she would come and help in here.'

Claire got up and went round the desk, but Scott Carver had reached the door before her. He didn't open it immediately, but stood for a moment with his fingers around the handle, and she got her first real look at his face. He was almost too handsome, the streaky fair hair complemented by tanned skin and deep blue eyes, a straight masculine nose and a square chin.

He studied her with undisguised interest, his eyes raking her face with a look of faint surprise before he opened the door for her and let her through.

The seaman was admitted to the hospital, and the yacht stayed anchored in the lagoon, a source of fascination to the islanders and for some reason a cause of mild irritation in Claire. The next day the children were distracted by squeals and laughter from the vessel, and then hugely entertained by the sight of a couple of bikini-clad young women and three even more scantily dressed men chasing one another about the deck, and then diving into the blue water of the lagoon, where the squeals and shouts and mirth continued until they returned to the boat.

Soon afterwards, however, a rowboat left the yacht and made for the shore, and when it beached, a group of people got out. They looked about at the huddle of mission buildings with the long corrugated iron copra shed behind them, and the nearby village made up of the islanders' simple thatched dwellings or more sophisticated but uglier houses with packing-case walls and corrugated iron roofs. Small children toddled about, watched by their mothers, who sat outside the houses weaving baskets and mats or painting designs on pieces of tapa cloth. The visitors stared for a few minutes and then turned slightly to look at the school. The children, consumed with curiosity, were by now totally unaware of Claire's attempts to keep their attention.

She gave up and yielded to her own curiosity. She could see at once that Scott Carver was not in the group. There were three young women—a blonde, a tall, striking brunette and a flaming redhead. They all had lovely figures and golden tans, even the redhead, though hers was more creamy and not as deep. And, in spite of the casual shorts and brief tops they wore, they all exuded an indefinable air of money. The three men with them had the same aura, although they were physically dissimilar. One was short and stocky, with a thick mat of dark hair covering his chest and arms, while the other two were taller, one of them red-haired and freckled, and one dark and flamboyantly handsome, though carrying a shade too much weight.

They appeared to be having some sort of discussion, but the tall dark man looked about, saw Claire watching them, and after a moment simply left his companions and began to walk through the scattered coconut palms toward the school.

The others followed him, talking loudly among themselves.

The man reached the school and leaned a hand on one of the posts supporting the thatch. Claire pushed her hair back from her eyes and said, 'Can I help you?'

He didn't answer immediately, but his insolent survey of her short, honey-coloured hair and clear green eyes, neat white dress, flat sandals and bare tanned legs, made her prickle with anger. He was undressing her mentally and making no effort to hide it. He smiled at her with conscious charm and said, 'I hope so. . . .' The pause was deliberate, before he added, 'What are you doing here?'

He didn't need to add, 'a pretty girl like you.' It was there in his eyes, in his smile, in the skeptical lift of his eyebrows.

Claire stiffened, her eyes cold. 'Teaching school,' she said briefly.

The others had caught up with him, and the blond girl, smiling delightedly, cried in a high-pitched voice, 'Oh, aren't they sweet? I just adore the little native kids! They're so cute! Don't you think they're cute, Jess?' She turned to the dark girl, who looked sardonically at her and shrugged.

The redheaded girl said, 'You think monkeys are cute, too, Sheryl.'

'Most of them understand English,' Claire said swiftly.

The girl looked at her with a flicker of surprise, as if one of the palm trees had just started talking, and Claire tried to fight off a wave of acute dislike.

The blonde knelt down and put out her arms to one of the smaller children, but the little boy shyly scuttled behind an elder brother sitting next to him and hid his face.

The girl laughed, and her friends joined in. Some of the children giggled in sympathy, and one edged closer to the visitors and put out a dusky hand to touch the blond girl's sleek hair.

The first man said to Claire, 'It's time we introduced ourselves. I'm Felix Holt. This is Morris, Doug, Darlene, Sheryl, Jess.'

Morris was the shorter dark man. Doug was the redheaded one, and she gathered that the girl who adored native children was Sheryl. The redhead was called Darlene, and Jess was the tall, green-eyed brunette.

She mustered a stiff smile, then said, 'My name's Claire. We're working, I'm afraid, so unless there's something I can do for you . . . ?'

She flushed at the unmistakable meaning in Felix's smile as he said, *sotto voce*, 'Well, now that you mention it . . .'

'Don't tease the girl,' the dark-haired Jess drawled in a smoky, amused voice. 'You are a menace, Felix!'

'You flatter me,' Felix said smugly, turning his attention to Jess. 'I wouldn't hurt a fly.'

'No, but then, it isn't flies that interest you, is it,

darling?' the girl challenged him, her eyes boldly
flirting.

Felix laughed, his survey of her frankly sexual, and
said, 'You know something about teasing yourself,
Jess. One of these days . . .'

'Oh, promises, promises!' she taunted, and then
dodged and ran from him as he moved with mock-
menace towards her.

The others turned and watched the pursuit, the
men shouting encouragement, the redhaired Darlene giggling. Jess made for the beach and ran into
the shallows, scooping up water to splash Felix as he
caught up with her. When he grabbed for her, she
ran back up the beach again, but he captured her
and wrestled her, laughing, down onto the sand.
Their legs were entangled, and as she lay on her
back with him on top of her, he bent his dark head
over hers and kissed her.

Morris and Doug cheered ironically, and Claire
glanced at her pupils, who were wide-eyed and
rather puzzled. When she looked back at the couple
on the beach, they were still kissing, and the girl's
arms had come up to wind themselves around the
man's neck.

Then she pushed against his chest, twisted away
and came upright in one lithe movement, laughing
down at Felix as he lay smiling back at her for a
moment before rising to his feet himself. He slipped
an arm about her waist as they walked back towards
the school.

Doug glanced at Claire's set face, grinned as
though something about her was funny, and said to
the others, 'I think we're disrupting the school day.
Come on, let's go.' At that they trooped off to join

the other two. The whole group wandered down the beach shortly afterwards and they were soon out of sight.

Later that day Claire had a further cause for concern when she found two of her pupils playing marbles, using the round seeds of the Alexandrian laurels that grew near the shore, but playing for money—Australian coins.

'Where did you get the money?' she asked, frowning. There was very little cash on the island; most trade was conducted by barter, and children were never given pocket money.

'Fella longa boat,' was the answer, accompanied by a gesture pointing to the yacht rocking gently at its anchorage.

'What did he give you money for?'

Much giggling and a confused story followed, but she gathered that one of the women from the yacht had asked some children to pose for a photograph, and the man with her had afterwards tossed them a few coins. She didn't like the idea, but told herself there was no cause for worry in someone giving a child a few cents.

The mission staff, excepting whoever was on duty in the ward, shared their evening meal in the kitchen-cum-dining-room attached to the hospital. That evening Sister Amy was the one on duty. Father Damien asked the other nurse, Sister Loretta, 'How's our patient from the yacht?'

'Better, but not much. The antibiotics aren't working as quickly as we had hoped.' Her smooth young brow puckered in a frown. 'Mr. Carver has been sitting with him most of the day. He's very concerned.'

'Yes, he was there when I visited the ward this morning. Interesting bloke. He captains the yacht himself, you know, seems quite an experienced sailor—ocean racing and that. Told me he was once on an expedition in the New Guinea Highlands—headhunting country.'

Claire was surprised. 'I thought he was one of the idle rich.'

'Oh, I should think he's rich, all right,' Father Damien said casually. 'But hardly idle. He's been around a bit. Africa, South America. He's done some tough trekking, I gather.'

He sounded slightly envious, and Claire wondered if a yen for travel was part of the reason that this young and rather brilliant priest had volunteered for a mission station serving several tiny islands in a remote corner of the Pacific.

Sister Martha, older than the others, a tough, whippy woman with a trenchant sense of humour, said, 'Well, from what I saw of those young women he's brought with him, I shouldn't think he'd have to go far to find a scalp-hunter or two. They were admiring the hospital garden, and the carroty one practically had poor old Jacob standing on his head.'

Jacob, the self-appointed mission gardener, had come in from one of the outlying islands some years before with a nasty gash on his leg and another on his face which had cost him an eye. The wounds had been inflicted by an outraged husband whose wife had attracted Jacob's illicit attentions, and after they had healed he had not dared return to his home for fear of further retribution. His hair was grizzled now, and he walked with a limp, but he was still a handsome figure of a man, although he swore he was a reformed character, a good Christian and a celibate emulating the examples of Saint Paul and Father Damien.

The picture of Jacob determinedly resisting the charms of the sophisticated young women from the yacht seemed irresistibly funny to them all, but amid the laughter Sister Loretta said, mock-severely, 'Charity, Sister Martha!'

'The good Lord forgive me!' Sister Martha murmured, raising her eyes. 'Am I lacking in charity?'

'Of course not!' Father Damien said warmly. 'You're the soul of kindness with the sick.'

'Ah, but it's easy to love the sick, Father.'

'Not for all of us.'

'No? For me it's not hard.' She grimaced. 'That sounds so saintly. But I'm not a saintly person at all. I wonder if it's just my bossy nature? Do I love the sick because they're too weak to stand up to me, perhaps? Goodness me, what a motive!'

Father Damien smiled. 'I'm sure the Lord knows all about your motives, Sister, and that He understands, whatever they are.'

'Oh, it might be better if He didn't understand!'

'We don't believe that.' Father Damien's smile included the other nun and Claire in his statement. 'It's doubtful if anyone's motives are completely pure, but you've done a great deal of good here, and I've no doubt the Lord is pleased about that.'

'Ah, but . . . what about Saint Paul? "Though I speak with the tongues of men and of angels, and hath not charity, I am no more than a sounding brass, or clashing cymbals?"'

'Surely that implies that kindness in deeds is more

important than anything you say?' the priest suggested.

Claire's mind drifted away from the rather light-hearted theological discussion that followed. Sister Loretta, smiling, her eyes bright with mischievous interest, leaned forward and took an eager part, teasing both Sister Martha and the priest, and Claire looked at her with a stirring of envy. Loretta was hardly older than herself, but she had combined her novitiate with her nursing studies, and made her final vows as a nun soon after gaining her nurse's stripes. Claire had not been so sure of her goals, so perhaps she ought to have understood the mother superior's hesitation over her request, back in Sydney, to be allowed to join the order. . . .

'I'm not sure, my dear,' the superior had said kindly, 'that you truly have a vocation for the religious life.'

'But, Mother Josephine, *I* am! I'm twenty-four. Old enough to know what I want.'

'What *you* want?' the nun had chided gently.

Claire flushed. 'I'm sure it's what God wants of me,' she insisted. 'I know that it's a late vocation—'

'Not so very,' Mother Josephine murmured. 'And that isn't necessarily a bad thing. Perhaps girls should know what it is they're giving up before they renounce the world.'

'Well, I do! I've been to university, to teachers' college, and I've held a job. I've even dated a few men. Not that I . . . I mean . . .'

The nun smiled. 'Of course, I know what you mean, Claire.'

'Well, then . . .'

Mother Josephine's brows rose. 'You think you are eligible to be a bride of Christ, is that it?'

The old romantic term, that Claire had read in the shabby biographies of the saints in the convent school's library, sounded strange on the lips of Mother Josephine, with her modern blue knee-length frock, her nylons and medium-heeled shoes, and the quite becoming dark blue veil that allowed a few rather attractive auburn curls to peep from beneath its narrow white edge. But she was a nun, and she wore a wedding ring on her third finger in token of her dedication to God, just as the pale saints in their starched wimples and voluminous habits had in earlier times.

'I know I'm not worthy,' Claire said humbly. 'But then . . .'

'Yes. Which of us is?'

'Then, please . . .'

Mother Josephine looked thoughtful. 'I've known you for a long time, Claire.'

'Yes, of course.' Mother Josephine had been a novice herself when Claire, a bewildered and unhappy eight-year-old, had been deposited in the convent orphanage by her mother. Perhaps because she was the youngest of the nuns, it was Josephine who had first managed to coax a smile from Claire, and who had gradually brought her out of her depths of sullen despair.

'You were a good child . . .'

'Oh, I know I wasn't!' Claire admitted ruefully.

'Of course you were. A handful sometimes, admittedly, once you found your feet, but you were never malicious or destructive.'

'Just bad-tempered.'

'Not really. Those rages of yours were understandable, in the circumstances. You could be stubborn, though.'

'Pigheaded,' Claire suggested.

Mother Josephine laughed. 'Perhaps. I always thought that your determination, channelled in the right direction, would be an asset to you someday.'

'I'm not so sure about that,' Claire said with slight bitterness.

There was a short silence. Then Mother Josephine said quietly, 'You have had a disappointment, I know.'

'You tried to warn me.'

'Yes, but you might have been right after all. It was something you had to find out for yourself in the end.'

'But you knew what she was like. That she'd never loved me.'

'My dear! I can't judge whether your mother ever loved you. She cried when she left you here with us, and when she visited she seemed very fond of you.'

'*But* . . . I can hear a "but" in your voice.'

Mother Josephine sighed. 'Some people are capable of only very shallow loving, I think,' she said finally. 'Your mother would have been quite young when she had you, and it couldn't have been easy for her as a single girl with a baby. She did keep you for eight years, after all.'

'Until she met Pietro Benotti.'

The nun's face clouded with compassion. 'Yes, well, as your mother explained it, she was in a dilemma. It must have been a great temptation to her—being offered marriage by a handsome and wealthy young man after years of struggling in low-paying jobs, with a daughter to support all on her own.'

'Tell me something, Mother. What did you think of the condition that he made? Marriage—if she would give up her daughter?'

Mother Josephine said slowly, 'It was monstrous, of course.' She paused. 'Did you . . . ever meet him?'

'No. Never. She told me about him, how wonderful he was, how rich. . . . She never brought him home. She would leave me with a sitter and go into the city to meet him. Then one day she came home so excited and showed me the ring he had given her—an enormous diamond. I've hated diamonds ever since,' Claire added irrelevantly. 'And then she said that he wanted her to himself for a while, like a sort of extended honeymoon. And she brought me here. It wasn't permanent, she said. She promised!'

For a moment her voice held an echo of a childish wail, and she swallowed, trying to be calm. 'You know, when she first used to come to see me, she talked of her new home, how big it was and how many pictures there were, and how much lovely antique furniture. . . . She said that one day I could go and live with them. It was always one day . . . soon . . . later. She said he was too busy to come and see me, but that he would love me when I came to live with them. And it was all untrue. One day I got upset and started crying, begging her to take me home, and then she told me that he . . . he didn't want me at all. He'd wanted to marry her, but he wouldn't take on another man's illegitimate child.'

The nun's face was softened. 'You weren't so very unhappy here with us, were you, Claire?'

'That's not the point!' For a moment she was shaken with the same ungovernable rage which had made her 'a handful' as a child. She got up from the wooden chair and walked over to the window, looking out onto the wide lawns where in her years of living here she had often played. She took three deep breaths to steady herself, her hands clenched on the small purse she carried. 'She refused to see me, you know,' she said to the shiny glass pane. 'When I tracked her down and rang up, asked if I could come round, she said she had hoped never to see me again and hung up on me.'

'Oh, my dear!' Mother Josephine got up and came to put an arm about Claire's shoulders. 'That was cruel. I expect it was partly shock. It must have been something of a surprise for her.' She wished the girl would turn to her, weep on her shoulder, allow herself to be comforted. But Claire kept looking out the window, her eyes dry and wide open.

'Oh, yes,' she said. 'It was a surprise. An unpleasant one, she made no bones about that.'

'I knew that the reunion hadn't been a success,' Mother Josephine said, 'but you didn't tell me this when I asked about it.'

'I was too raw then. I've had a couple of months to get over it now.'

'You don't think she might have changed her mind once she got over the initial shock?'

'I wrote to her and gave her the address of the flat where I'm living now. She hasn't even bothered to reply.'

Mother Josephine summoned all her training in self-discipline and charity to quell a surge of fury. Years ago she had prayed for understanding, or at least acceptance, when it became clear that Gail Wyndham-Benotti had finally abandoned her daughter. It was not so uncommon for parental visits to cease, gradually or suddenly, but Claire had come to the orphanage later than most of their charges and had been living on promises for many months. Sister Josephine, as she was then, had always found it difficult to relate to Gail, who was artificially refined and genuinely silly. Quite quickly it had become apparent that she had always been a somewhat erratic mother, and she had one day admitted to Sister Josephine that when she had decided to keep her baby girl, because she was 'too cute and pretty to part with,' she hadn't had the faintest idea how to look after her or how they were to live. Claire's rapid growth from a relatively placid baby to a lively and sometimes demanding little girl had taken her unawares, and she alternated between resentment of the responsibility and sentimental, guilt-ridden loving. After eight years the advent of Pietro Benotti seemed almost too good to be true, and she had, Sister Josephine gathered, set out to milk the wealthy Italian-Australian of all she could get. When the infatuated Pietro had actually suggested marriage she had been ecstatic, but it was evident to Sister Josephine that the most overriding thought in her mind had been what to do about her embarrassing daughter.

Sister Josephine had at first accepted, along with everyone else, the story that Mr. Benotti could not face the thought of having his wife's illegitimate child in his home, but that Gail hoped to bring him round to the idea in time. Sister Josephine reasoned that it was easy for a celibate nun to believe that she herself would never have accepted marriage on those terms; marriage was not her vocation, and she had no right to pass judgment. She had even held her tongue when Claire innocently repeated her mother's assertions that Pietro was looking forward to welcoming her into his family. After all, it could do the child no good to know that her mother's new husband had rejected her, especially if he did later change his mind.

But Sister Josephine began to suspect strongly that the husband's opposition was a fiction, and the whole story fabricated to excuse Gail for putting her child in a children's home while she enjoyed her new wealth and prestige unencumbered by any reminder of her past life. The cessation of Gail's visits hadn't surprised any of the sisters, but the young Sister Josephine had felt bound to confess to some fiercely uncharitable thoughts in regard to Mrs. Benotti.

Now Mother Josephine didn't know if the truth would help or hinder Claire's recovery from heartache. But, feeling that enough lies had been told to the girl, and believing that truth was an overriding principle, she said, 'Claire, I've sometimes doubted that Mr. Benotti ever did make that condition.'

Claire was silent for a long time. Then she said, 'Of course,' as though it was something she had always known, really, or should have known, and now accepted without any particular feeling. 'She never even told him about me, did she?'

Mother Josephine tightened her arm on the drooping shoulders she still held. 'It must have been hard for her,' she said. 'I don't know if you realise—

she was pregnant when she stopped coming here. Quite noticeably pregnant.'

'Oh.' Claire struggled to absorb that. 'You mean, she was pregnant when she married Mr. Benotti? Do you think that's why he asked her to marry him?'

'I think it's possible.'

'He was offering to make an honest woman of her. Yes, I do see,' Claire said harshly. 'It would have been rather difficult, under the circumstances, to suddenly confront him with the . . . evidence of an earlier illegitimate pregnancy. Wouldn't it?'

'I imagine she would have felt so,' Sister Josephine said gently. 'We can't know what she was going through at the time.'

'You're very forgiving,' Claire muttered, turning away so that the nun's arm slipped from her shoulders.

Mother Josephine smiled sadly. 'I'm not the child she abandoned,' she said. 'You are. Can you forgive her?'

Claire shut her eyes. 'You know the answer. I've tried. I really have tried. But I don't think I can. Is that why you won't accept me? It's a flaw, isn't it? Seventy times seven, one should forgive, it says in the Bible. I can't even forgive once. I hate her. I shouldn't say that. It's a sin to hate, isn't it? I suppose you're right; I'm not good enough for the order.'

'That isn't why,' Mother Josephine told her firmly. She returned to her seat behind the rosewood desk in the visitors' parlour. 'None of us is perfect, and at the moment the latest rejection, the hurt, is too new. Forgiveness may come in time. You must pray that it does. Not just for her sake, but for yours, for your own peace of mind.'

Claire brushed that aside. 'If it isn't that,' she said, 'why won't you take me as a postulant? You know this isn't the first time I've asked. I've always loved it here.'

'The order is worldwide, Claire. If you joined you might not be allowed to stay here. The superior general could transfer you at any time.'

That was a slight shock. But Claire braced herself quickly and said, 'Yes, well, I'll cross that bridge when I come to it.'

Mother Josephine smiled. She recognised very clearly the stubborn set of the girl's chin, the glow of determination in her eyes. Even when she was a child it had been unwise to risk a head-on confrontation with Claire in this mood.

'Last time you asked to join us,' she pointed out, 'you were very young—only fifteen.'

'And you told me it was a stage many girls pass through at that age—the ultrareligious phase. You said to ask again in a few years' time if I still felt the same.'

'It's been nine years, Claire.'

'I still feel the same.'

'That's what I'm afraid of,' the mother superior sighed.

'I don't understand you! Vocations are declining; you *know* how few girls are going into religious life nowadays. I should think you'd jump at the chance of getting one. It isn't as though I'm committing myself utterly—if you're right, and it isn't for me, I'll find out in the novitiate, surely? Or even in the initial stage, when I'm only a postulant. The order gives me four years to make up my mind before taking my final vows.'

'Yes, I know. But I know you, too, Claire. You wouldn't give up once you'd set your hand to the plough. I'm afraid that you don't have a true vocation, but that you'd choose to ignore that once you had committed yourself in your own mind, no matter that the convent gates were still wide open.'

'*Why* are you so sure I don't have a vocation?' Claire stormed, her cheeks flaming with angry colour. Then Sister Josephine gave her an old-fashioned look, and she sank back into her chair, biting her lip. 'I'm sorry.'

Sister Josephine shook her head admonishingly. 'I'm not sure, of course,' she said. 'But I do have some experience—of you, and of the religious life. Do you want me to be honest?'

'Yes.' The syllable came out clipped, crisp.

'Very well. I think that when you were fifteen, as well as being at an intensely religious, mystical stage, you were a little scared of being nearly old enough to leave us and go out into the world. You were brought up here; it was your home. I didn't feel that it would be right to let you stay in the nest forever. You had to be encouraged to try your wings, even if eventually they brought you back here. We can't take frightened children into the order. We need adults here who can cope with a demanding and sometimes hard life of self-sacrifice, a total giving of oneself to others—and, through others, to God.'

Huskily Claire said, 'I'm not a child now. You said you were afraid my reasons were still the same.'

'Yes. I think that you're here because you've been hurt again, rejected again, by your mother. I think that what you're looking for is a refuge, a place to hide away and lick your wounds. I'm afraid you're thinking less of what you can give than of what you need. It isn't the attitude I look for in postulants. Religious life is not a cushion, Claire. It's a challenge.'

Claire winced, her face whitening.

'I don't mean to hurt you, my dear,' the nun said gently. 'But you must be honest with yourself.'

Claire swallowed. 'I'm trying. I don't think you're right. I . . . Perhaps there is some truth in that, but, please . . . give me a chance. I promise that if I realise I'm wrong I'll leave.'

Sister Josephine regarded her hands which were clasped on the desk in front of her. 'I wonder,' she said slowly, 'if you would consider something. . . .'

'What?'

'Our order has three sisters on a small mission station in the Solomons. One native sister and two Australians, and a priest. The sisters are nurses— two of them are qualified and the other is a lay sister—and they have a hospital there, but they badly need a teacher. The need is urgent, since they have been without one for six months now. Will you spend a year with the sisters and teach in the mission school? And if at the end of that time you still want to enter the convent, I shall be very pleased to recommend to the order your acceptance as a postulant.'

Her first instinct had been to say no, she wanted to start her training then, not wait another year. Then she remembered that a few minutes earlier the mother superior had said she wanted postulants who thought of what they could give to the order, to God, rather than of what their own needs were. It was an effort, but she saw it as her first lesson in religious obedience. 'Yes,' she said. 'I will.'

Chapter Two

Working on the island had been an experience she would never forget. The setting was idyllic. The coral atoll was surrounded by the crystal water of a lagoon teeming with colourful tropical fish, bordered by dazzling white beaches and fringed with coconut palms and coastal trees. Inland were plantations of bananas, tapioca, yam and taro, the islanders' staple foods, and a mass of uncultivated land covered in lush rain forest.

The people were shy but friendly, even those who had not accepted the missionaries' teaching and still clung to old gods and strangely carved black wooden idols. The children were a delight to teach, quick and eager to learn, and she had passed on some of her teaching skills to islanders in the other two villages, and also to some people from the other islands in the group within the mission's province. She liked feeling that she was helping the islanders, and she felt privileged to take part in the spiritual life of the missionaries, attending Father Damien's early Mass every morning with the sisters and being allowed to join them for evening prayers. The slow pace they of necessity adopted in the humid heat brought her a serenity that had been difficult to achieve in Sydney, teaching in a large city school and living first in a hostel and then in an apartment with two other young teachers.

Nor was she quite deprived of the company of her own age group. She and the younger nun had taken to each other from the first, and in private Loretta had asked her to dispense with the title of 'Sister.'

Father Damien sometimes forgot it, too, but Loretta was always careful to address him very correctly, although he was not much older than herself and never stood on ceremony. They all worked as a team, with little sense of hierarchy, but Sister Martha and Sister Amy, trained in more formal times, were inclined to accord the priest a deference that he obviously found rather embarrassing. The nearest he could bring them to friendly informality was to get them to combine the title of Father with his Christian name rather than his surname.

There were young women, of course, among the people of the island, but they married in their teens and by the time they reached their twenties were preoccupied with growing families and domestic chores. There were gardens to be cultivated, pigs and poultry to be tended, shellfish to be gathered in the rock pools, paper mulberry bark to be soaked and pounded and dried and turned into tapa cloth for clothing or for partitions in the simple houses, and mats, baskets and hats to be woven from the leaves of pandanus and coconut trees. Claire was constantly amazed at the busy energy of the young matrons who, in spite of their many tasks, sang while they worked and always seemed to wear cheerful smiles.

If her own life was a contrast to theirs, the lives of the three young women who had arrived on Scott Carver's yacht were even more so. The lights on board were still blazing when Claire went to bed, and the sounds of laughter and music and even the clinking of glass on glass carried clearly across the lagoon. Claire's small room looked out over the water, and she stood at the open window for several minutes, watching and listening, her thoughts oddly troubled and confused, before she slid between the cool cotton sheets. She remembered the quick rush of antagonism she had felt when the group had approached the school and Sheryl had declared her love of 'native' children, as though they were kittens or puppies.

The girl couldn't help it, she told herself. She had meant well, and it wasn't her fault if her patronising attitude had set Claire's teeth on edge.

And then the other two, kissing so blatantly on the beach in front of all the children. Of course Claire had seen people behaving in a similar fashion on the beaches back home, at Bondi and Manly. But it was out of place here. Even their bikinis were out of place on the island. The native women might have gone bare-breasted once, but now they wore colourful and modest dresses of bright printed cotton, trimmed with snow-white lace at the cuffs and necklines, and sometimes at the hemline, too. And if they swam they donned a kind of sarong wrapped about them and secured under the arms.

Claire hadn't swum that night. Most evenings she had a dip in the lagoon, wearing one of the local sarongs over her own rather modest bikini. But the beach was in full view of the yacht, and she hadn't fancied being watched by the visitors. The next day would be Saturday and there was no school. She might go for a walk in the afternoon and find a more private place farther around the island and out of sight.

The yacht, anchored only a couple of hundred yards offshore, still attracted some attention from the children the next day as they splashed about in the lagoon, enjoying their day off from school. The blonde and the redhead—Sheryl and Darlene, Claire remembered, watching from the shade of the hospital veranda, where she sat with a book—came out on deck before midday and sunbathed on top of the wheelhouse. When she saw Sheryl sit up and remove her top Claire went hot with annoyance, but the children squealing and running about on the beach and in the shallows didn't appear to notice. She only hoped that the visitors would at least have the sense to keep their minimal clothes on the next time they left the yacht for the island.

One of the men came out on deck sometime later and wandered over to lean on the wheelhouse and talk to the girls. Darlene had now discarded her top, too, and she was sitting up anointing her breasts with, presumably, suntan oil. She handed the bottle to the man—it must have been Scott Carver; he was tall and fair—and turned over on her stomach while he smoothed the stuff over her back.

With an effort Claire wrenched her gaze back to her book and tried to concentrate on the pages of *The Life and Times of St. Paul.*

She saw Scott Carver at closer quarters afterwards. He walked past the window of the clinic while she was helping Sister Amy with a child who had burnt his foot wandering into a fire, and she guessed he was visiting the sick crewman. He didn't glance at her and there was no one with him, but in the late afternoon when Claire was talking with some of the young women in the shade cast by one of the huts, she saw that Morris, Doug, Sheryl and Darlene had come ashore. A group of children was dogging the footsteps of the party, and Doug, the redheaded man, threw a handful of coins on the sand. The children scrambled to pick them up, the victorious ones dancing with glee as they held the shiny rounds of metal high above their heads. The visitors laughed and passed on.

They strolled into the village and came over to the hut, and the native women smiled shyly, greeting them and inviting them to share the mats they and Claire were sitting on. Morris, surveying Claire interestedly, said, 'Hello, Claire,' while the others gave her a casual 'Hi.'

Darlene, Claire thought, had a bored expression on her face, but she shrugged and accepted the women's invitation to sit down, and Doug followed, leaning a forearm on her shoulder.

The blond Sheryl looked at the mats and said doubtfully, 'Well, they *look* clean enough, I suppose,' but hesitated until Morris ostentatiously took a handkerchief from one pocket of the faded cutoff jeans which were all he was wearing and facetiously dusted the woven pandanus for her.

Claire flushed with shame and anger. The island women were very houseproud and would never have dreamed of inviting a visitor to sit on a mat that was anything less than spotless.

They also, she thought, had better manners than their guests. Nothing was said; only their marked silence and the lowering of their dark eyes to their work gave any hint of their feelings.

Apparently quite unaware of having committed any gaffe, Sheryl looked curiously at the deft fingers of a woman who was plaiting stiff coconut leaves in and out, fashioning an intricately designed large shallow tray. 'Is it nearly finished?' she asked, speaking slowly and loudly, apparently under the impression that 'natives' were universally deaf.

The woman nodded, slanting her a smile.

'Very pretty,' Sheryl shouted. 'How much?'

The island woman was nonplussed. She was probably making the tray for her family or as a gift for a relative.

'*How . . . much?*' Sheryl repeated, more loudly still.

'Four, five day,' the woman said finally, shrugging.

'What?' Sheryl looked helplessly at Morris as though it was his job as a man to come to the rescue.

'That's how long it takes to make, I guess,' he said. He glanced at Claire, who sat in deliberate silence. A flicker of something that might have been a kind of understanding came and went in his eyes.

Sheryl followed his gaze and said almost accusingly to Claire, 'You said they speak English.'

'I said most of the children understand English,' Claire corrected her. 'This lady does, too, but not every word.'

Doug snickered softly and exclaimed, *'Lady!'* Darlene giggled and punched him covertly in the ribs, saying, 'Shh!' And Sheryl said impatiently to Claire, 'Well, ask her what she wants for the tray, will you?'

Claire took a moment to control her irritation and remind herself that tolerance was a virtue to be cultivated. Then she turned and explained in her limited pidgin that the visiting lady wanted to buy the tray.

The brown face lit up immediately with delighted comprehension. 'Ah . . . ah!' the woman said. 'How many dollah?'

A look of what Claire tried not to describe to herself as low cunning came into Sheryl's pretty, vapid face. 'How many dollars you want?' she asked.

The matron shrugged and looked round at her companions, who also shrugged and laughed. She returned her attention to the work in her fingers for a few moments, tying off a knot and picking up a knife to cut the last untidy threads. She looked at the finished product, held it out to Sheryl and said, apparently at random, 'T'ree dollah?'

'That's less than a dollar per day's work—' Claire interjected.

But Sheryl said shrewdly, 'How about two dollars?'

The woman looked abashed. Bargaining was the norm in many tourist islands, but here it was not known. Trying not to show embarrassment at having asked too much, she nodded eagerly. 'Two dollah okay.'

'Morris . . .' Sheryl turned to the man at her side, and he laughed and pulled out a wallet.

'Thanks, darling, I'll pay you back later,' Sheryl told him.

From the long-suffering look he gave her, Claire deduced that he doubted that, but he handed over two notes to the craftswoman, who studied them interestedly.

'You gave her too much, you fool!' Sheryl said, snatching one of them back. 'Two dollars, I said.'

She handed the note back to Morris, who said patiently, 'Oh, let her have the four dollars. You can pay me two.'

'That's not the point!' Sheryl pouted. 'I bargained for this tray, and you're spoiling my bargain.'

Morris took the note and closed his fist around it. 'Okay,' he said easily. 'Is anyone else buying?'

Apparently they weren't. Darlene and Doug were getting to their feet, and Sheryl jumped up to join them, clutching her purchase. They moved away without a good-bye or a word of thanks, but Morris hesitated a moment, tossed the crumpled note down on the woven mat in front of the tray-maker, winked at Claire and went after his companions.

The woman looked at the note for almost a minute before she picked it up and tucked it away with the other in the sleeve of her dress.

Claire got up shortly afterwards and made her way to the little church. She was blindly angry. It wasn't any way for a would-be nun to feel, and she hoped that a half-hour of prayer and meditation would ease her mood.

But God seemed far away from her today. All she managed to achieve was a restless frustration in the place of pure rage. In the end she went for a long walk along one of the meandering tracks between the coconut groves and banana plantations that covered the centre of the island. She needed a mountain, or at least a decent-sized hill, to climb, she thought. But the island wasn't a volcanic cone, only a low atoll a few feet above sea level. All she could do was keep walking to exhaustion and then cool off with a swim in the lagoon. She passed a family group working on their banana plantation, the father making fenceposts to keep out marauding pigs, using a huge machete with delicate precision to sharpen the stakes, the mother and children gathering green bananas for cooking. They waved and she called out a greeting and went on.

Sometime later she came upon a group of ancient trees within sight of the sea, their branches sweeping the sandy ground, their great trunks gnarled and twisted, making a series of hollows and humps and dark recesses hidden under the undulating green canopy of leaves.

She heard a muted scrabbling, and made to beat a hasty retreat. Coconut crabs, huge creatures that climbed the palms and sent the coconuts crashing to the ground to smash open and expose their sweet white flesh to the predators, inhabited parts of the shoreline and sometimes came quite far inland. They weren't normally dangerous to humans, but she didn't want to stumble on one, all the same.

In her haste to escape she fell backwards over a protruding root and went flying to the ground.

Immediately gurgles of imperfectly stifled childish laughter came from nearby, and she picked herself up, dusted down her dress and looked about for the source of them.

Some leaves several feet off the ground rustled and quivered, and she went closer, calling, 'I hear you . . . hello?'

More giggles, but no sign of any children.

Curious, she climbed onto a low branch, peering upwards. A black cavelike hollow, formed by several trunks growing almost in a circle and in their growth joined together, met her eyes.

Smiling, she guessed that some children had claimed it for a hidey-hole. Well, she would let them keep their secret. Ready to climb down again, she was stopped by the sudden appearance of one of her school pupils at the entrance to the hollow.

'Hello, Munda,' she said.

''Ullo, miss. You coma longa see?'

The little girl beckoned, and after a moment's hesitation Claire nodded. 'Thank you.'

It wasn't difficult to make the remainder of the climb. The thick trunks and branches were smooth except for some irregular patches of lifting bark with hard edges which she avoided. Munda scuttled backwards, and Claire, bending, was able to follow her and see that Munda's sister Tana was squatting farther back in the recess, which was seven or eight feet long, about half as wide in the middle and narrow at each end.

As her eyes became accustomed to the gloom she

made out the shabby pandanus matting on the 'floor,' which was surprisingly flat and slightly spongy, formed, Claire supposed, by decades of debris that had fallen or been blown into the fork of the joined trees. Some coconut halves, shells and a carved miniature canoe were arranged on a natural shelf formed by a convolution of the trees.

'Our house,' Munda explained.

'It's lovely,' Claire told them.

'Secret house,' Tana said, putting a brown finger to her lips.

'I understand. I won't tell anyone,' Claire promised.

Tana scrambled to her feet. 'Missy lika *kai-kai?*' she asked.

Wondering what sort of food they were offering, Claire said with some trepidation, 'Thank you. Just a little.'

Delighted to offer hospitality, they spread a small square of tapa cloth on the floor and placed on it some bits of coconut and small yellow fruit that she recognised as *wi*, the edible fruit of one of the local trees. It tasted something like apples, and she was able to sincerely tell them that she had enjoyed her snack before she left them, promising again to keep their secret.

The incident had distracted her and mellowed her mood, helping her to put things in perspective. Scott Carver, his friends and his yacht were only a temporary ripple on the surface of the tranquil island life. A few coins thrown to the children, a tactless remark here and there, would scarcely influence the future of the community. Soon they would be gone and the islanders would have hardly noticed their passing. And Claire, too, would forget she had ever met them.

In the end the walk had stretched so that she had no time left to find a secluded spot on the shore before helping with the evening meal in the hospital, so once more she had to forgo her swim, which made her cross again.

When she went into the ward Scott Carver was sitting by Eddie Robson's bed, but Sister Amy came in soon afterwards, while Claire was serving the first two patients, and he got up and went over to speak to her. The sister nodded understandingly at the concern on his face, and after a few moments they both went out.

On Sunday the islanders filled the simple church, some from the other villages miles away across the island, and others coming from atolls over the horizon in their double-hulled canoes. The cool, dim building took on life and colour as the islanders, both men and women wearing scented floral wreaths on their heads and dressed in their colourful Sunday best, harmonised the ancient Christian hymns translated into their own language. No one from the *Bella Donna* appeared in church, but when the congregation emerged into the brilliant sunlight the visitors could be seen lolling against the rails at her stern. Claire supposed that even if they weren't interested in the service, they had enjoyed the music.

The villagers kept a strict Sunday without work, spending the time visiting each other's homes, reading from the Bible, telling stories and singing. After lunch in the mission kitchen Claire put her bikini on under one of her cotton shirtwaister dresses, rolled up fresh undies in a sarong and, draping a large towel around her neck, set off along the gritty coral sand.

The water of the lagoon lapped at the shore, and the palm trees clacked faintly in a slight warm breeze. From the village the sounds of children playing and someone singing a chanting island song came through the trees, fading as she went farther along the sand.

A group of children was splashing about in the shallows, looking for fish in pockets of coral, lunging at them with their bare hands, squealing and laughing. They saw her and came running, calling, ''Ullo, miss; w'ere you goin', miss? Hey, you lika fella fish?' in a mixture of the English she tried to teach them and the local version of pidgin.

One of them had actually caught one of the darting lagoon fish, a small, luminous, struggling object held fast in bare brown hands.

'Oh,' she said, 'he's very little. Too small to eat, surely?'

The young fisherman shrugged. 'Yeah, we t'row 'um back, eh?'

Relieved, she nodded, and watched as they placed the tiny creature back in the lagoon with an oddly touching tenderness, moving their hands in the water to shoo it away and following its wriggling progress until it swam out of their depth.

Around the curve of the beach a clump of screw pines with their distinctive bunches of long, thin leaves grew at the water's edge, their strange aerial roots making passage difficult, and she had to walk under the coconut palms farther up before gaining the sand again. Now all was quiet, only the hiss of the water kissing the sand and the occasional screech of a parakeet breaking the silence. The ocean seemed to stretch limitlessly to the pale sky, a line of gold separating them as the sun caught the water.

She found a small sheltered bay where the sea had scooped a bite out of the land, fringed by spreading Alexandrian laurel trees with fragrant white flowers, and bushes of yellow hibiscus. The sand there was soft and powdery, lacking the harshness of the more exposed shores, and her feet sank into it gratefully.

An old twisted tree with a broad malformed trunk made a convenient shelter for stripping off her dress, and she picked up the sarong to don over the bikini, then hesitated. There was no one about to see, and it would be a pleasant change to feel the water against her skin. She rolled up the sarong and deposited it with her folded towel at the base of the tree, then ran into the water.

It was heavenly, caressing her body like liquid satin, a forgivable taste of natural luxury, surely. She dived under, picking up a speckled, spiral-shaped shell from the litter of dead coral and other shells on the bottom, and surfaced to examine her find. It was damaged at the tip, and regretfully she threw it away. There would be plenty of others. She had never been a collector, but the treasure that the sea yielded here was too tempting to ignore. Farther out there were great valleys in the seabed littered with dead and colourful living corals, where fat spotted sea slugs clung to the slopes, and bright yellow fish undulated between the rocks and the coral outcrops. The coral didn't retain its colour out of the sea, but she had at least two dozen lovely shells, each one perfect, in her room at the mission, and not the faintest idea what she was going to do with them when she got back to Australia. The order demanded poverty, chastity and obedience, and she would renounce the concept of ownership when she joined it. Of course, rules were not as strict as they had once been, and perhaps no one would object if she wanted to have one or two commercially valueless shells by her to remind her of the island, but having a collection was probably contrary to the spirit of poverty.

She turned on her back, floating and thinking about that new life, trying to picture herself in a nun's veil and habit, accepting the discipline of the rule, a life of prayer and service. But other pictures kept intruding—of a tall, fair man leaning over the girl Darlene and slowly caressing her back with his hand in long, sweeping strokes . . . and of Felix and Jess, kissing with abandon on the white coral sand, the girl's hands on the man's tanned shoulders, pink-tipped fingers spread against his skin.

No one had ever kissed Claire like that. She had never wanted them to. The few men she had gone out with had had to be content with a brief and friendly good-night kiss, if they were lucky. If they pressed too hard for more, she simply stopped seeing them. Casual sex was not for her. Although she had tried hard to concede that other people had a right to their own values, after being brought up in the sheltered environment of the convent she had never ceased to be rather shocked by the ready acceptance of sex without marriage among her contemporaries, and was frankly horrified by some of the books and magazines that they seemed to accept as depicting normal behaviour among certain social groups, particularly the rich and famous.

One of her friends had lent her a best-seller which made her mind reel with its graphically described sexual adventures, the plot consisting mainly of a sort of musical chairs of changing partners in combinations that seemed not only immoral but also highly unlikely.

When she had said so, her friend had laughed and said, 'You're too innocent to be true, Claire! Lots of people live like that. Everyone knows this story is based on real people. The author is one of them; that's how he gets his inside information. I've got a cousin in the oil business—at least her husband is. They've got pots of money and move with the world jet set. She swears it's true to life.'

'Well, maybe,' Claire had said doubtfully. 'It's certainly not the kind of life I want to lead.'

'Me either,' her friend had admitted, almost regretfully. 'All I want is one good man and a parcel of kids, though it's awfully dim to admit it, these days. But I wouldn't mind meeting a bloke like the racing driver in this book, just to have a short fling before I settle down.'

'You'd be one of a string,' Claire had pointed out. 'He sleeps with four different women in the course of the story and doesn't really care about any of them.'

'I wouldn't mind, as long as it was good while it lasted. Well, I can dream, can't I?'

Claire's dreams were of a different order. She had gone through a stage of wanting 'one good man and a parcel of kids' too. She liked children, and enjoyed teaching as a career. And although she had made a few good friends, and could always find a welcome at the convent when she visited, she was lonely for a family of her own.

She was attractive enough to gain a certain amount of male attention, but after having to fight off some unwelcome advances on one or two occasions she had become very selective and cautious. Even so, her heart had not remained untouched. She had fallen in love with one of her fellow students at the teachers' college, gone round with him for a while, and allowed him to kiss her when he took her back to the hostel at night. When he told her he loved her, too, and wanted her to move in with him, she had made too many assumptions too fast. It bothered her that he didn't share her religion, but when she mentioned it he had laughed incredulously and made it quite plain that whatever he meant by 'being together' and 'loving each other' did not include anything permanent enough to make their differing religious beliefs an issue. When she broke off the relationship, feeling foolish and ashamed of her naïveté, he had been thoroughly baffled and bewildered. Claire, however, had been too humiliated to explain.

The next object of her affection was a youth leader from her local church, a young man whose high ideals matched her own and who had taken her out many times. They had seemed soulmates, interested in the same things, enjoying the same jokes, and of course sharing the same church affiliation. They often attended Mass together on Sundays, and sometimes would go to confession before a Saturday night spent dancing or taking in a show in the city.

They kissed with frank warmth but restrained passion, and talked for hours about life, politics, ethics and religion. It was only later that Claire realised they had seldom, if ever, talked about themselves, about their private feelings and ambitions—after he told her in troubled tones that he was becoming too fond of her and that love and marriage didn't fit into his plans. He had been thinking for a long time of becoming a missionary brother, and was now sure of his call to vocation.

'But why did you take me out?' she had asked him, confused and hurt. 'That doesn't fit in with your plans either, does it?'

'Look, I've taken no vows yet,' he explained. 'And I wasn't sure. . . . I thought we could be friends, and . . . Well, I suppose it was a way of helping me to make up my mind. In some ways I hoped I was wrong about God wanting me to be a religious brother. There's a lot to give up. . . .'

'And you wanted to experience some of it before you did.'

'No! It wasn't like that. I liked you a lot. I thought maybe marriage was right for me after all. But . . . even when I realised I could fall in love with you, Claire, somehow I knew more and more clearly that marriage isn't for me. I'm sorry, I suppose it's hard to understand.'

'I want to,' she said at last. 'Only . . . I feel that you've just been using me—experimenting.'

'Darling . . .'

'Don't call me that! You don't have the right . . . do you?'

He bit his lip. 'I suppose not. I wasn't experimenting. I wish I could make you see how I feel.'

'I'm trying.'

'That's all I can ask. And I'm sorry if I've hurt you. It was the last thing I wanted to do, believe me.'

He kissed her before he went away, with passion. And then he said huskily, 'That wasn't an experiment either, Claire. I could have loved you—but as you said, I don't have the right. Be happy.'

She had not been happy; she had been hurt and lonely. It was soon afterwards that she made up her mind to trace her mother, who had gone away from Sydney with her husband sometime after ceasing to visit the orphanage. Although checks for Claire's keep had arrived somewhat erratically after that, Sister Josephine had told her, she had never given the sisters a forwarding address.

It had not been as difficult as Claire had expected to find out that her mother was living in Adelaide with her husband and two children. At first the fact of having half-brothers had been a peculiar shock. Later she had begun to look forward to meeting them. But the meeting had never taken place. Her mother had not wanted it.

Tears squeezed from beneath Claire's closed eyelids and mingled with the sea water on her cheeks as she lay, moving her hands and feet just enough to keep her afloat on the warm surface. Impatiently she shook off the gloomy thoughts and dived again, coming up to swim along the shoreline in an invigorating crawl designed to chase away introspection and self-pity.

It helped, and she came reluctantly out of the water as the tropical dusk began to creep from the trees at the sand's edge.

She made her way to the big old tree where she had left her things, picked up the towel to dry her hair and then dropped it to unhook the bra of her bikini and slide the straps down her arms.

'I should warn you that you're being watched,' said a male voice, making her jump and gasp in shock. Instinctively she swung round, making an ineffectual grab at the top. Then, realising that she was only affording the man a better view, she turned again, snatched up the towel and clutched it in front of her. When she faced in the direction of the voice once more she saw that he had been sitting in the crotch of the trunk of one of the nearby trees where it branched out, slightly above her eye level. He jumped lightly down, and she recognised Scott Carver.

He was grinning, obviously enjoying himself. His eyes were on her bare shoulders, skimming over the towel with amusement and down to her long, slim legs, which he eyed with appreciation.

Finding her voice, she demanded furiously, 'What do you think you're doing, you . . . you Peeping Tom!'

He looked at her face and she saw him frown slightly, as though something puzzled him. 'I did tell you I was here,' he said calmly, 'as soon as I realised you intended to undress.'

'You didn't need to watch!'

'I might have shut my eyes, but would you have believed that, if you'd got changed and then noticed me up there? I couldn't move discreetly away without you seeing me.'

She remained silent, acknowledging that he had a point. He came a couple of steps closer, looking intently at her face. The frown had deepened. 'I was watching you swim,' he said almost absently. Then she saw enlightenment and, surprisingly, embarrassment dawn on his face. His expression seemed to close down suddenly, and he said with unmistakable sincerity, 'I didn't realise who you were. I'm sorry, Sister. One doesn't expect . . . Look, I apologise, okay?'

He meant the apology, she could see that, but a quirk was tugging at the corner of his mouth, as though he had just seen the funny side of something.

Tongue-tied, Claire nodded jerkily, and he sketched a quick salute and turned away, murmuring, 'Good afternoon, then.'

She didn't answer, and for long moments after he had disappeared among the trees she stood with the towel stupidly held at her breasts, until she realised she was shivering in spite of the warm tropical evening, and began feverishly to dress.

She had allowed him to believe she was a nun, and the fact niggled at her conscience all the way back to the mission.

She supposed it had been a natural assumption. She was the only lay person on the mission staff, and he had previously only seen her in the simple cotton button-through dresses that resembled those the nuns wore, and with her hair covered by a white square of cloth.

Well, it was nearly true. In a month she would be returning to Australia, and she fully intended to enter the postulantship there. Her time on the island had made her more determined than ever to dedicate her life to the love of God and to helping others for His sake. She no longer wanted to find a man

who would give her his love and a home and family
of her own. The only safe, secure and constant love
was God's love, and her family would be all the
children she taught or cared for in the Order's
schools and children's homes. It would be a full life
and a satisfying one, and if it meant some self-
sacrifice, it meant also peace and protection from
pain.

What did it matter that it was not yet fact—that
Scott Carver had jumped to conclusions that were at
the moment unfounded? He wasn't important to
her, nor she to him. In a few days he would be gone
and the island would return to its normal tranquil-
lity.

When she entered the ward that evening Scott
Carver was there again with Eddie Robson. He got
up as she wheeled in the trolley from the kitchen,
and came over, saying, 'Can I help?'

The white cloth tied about her head and knotted
at the nape fell across her cheek as she took a plate
and ladled some of the rice, coconut and fish mixture
onto it. 'You might give that to Mr. Robson,' she
said. 'And tell him if he doesn't fancy island food,
Sister Martha will fix him something else.'

She handed it to him without looking at his face
and quickly turned to fill a second plate for one of
the other patients.

'I'm sure this will be fine,' he said. 'I know Eddie
likes island dishes—we've been eating native
throughout the Pacific.'

He stood there until she went to serve the man in
the nearest bed, and when she came back to the
trolley he was over with Eddie Robson, apparently
trying to coax him to eat. The crewman was still

listless and slightly feverish, with little appetite, but Claire was able to see that his employer, holding the plate for him, had talked him into trying the rice. He ate half of it before he shook his head and pushed away the dish.

Claire finished distributing the food, and helped an anxious mother, who had stayed by her fretful child all day, to persuade him to take a few mouthfuls of manioc custard.

Relatives were encouraged to help care for the patients in the hospital and were allowed to provide some food if it was suitable, though the main meal was cooked in the hospital kitchen. There were two private rooms where very ill or infectious people were kept quiet and isolated, but generally, Sister Amy believed, people recovered more quickly if they were allowed, as much as possible, to remain members of the gregarious and caring community that surrounded them. Curtains were sufficient to segregate age groups and sexes when necessary, but for most of the day the ward resembled a large, happy family such as most of the patients were accustomed to. There were no visiting hours and relatives came and went as they had the time or inclination, removing themselves cheerfully when the nurses or visiting doctor asked them to leave for a time so that the patient might receive treatment or rest.

Scott Carver brought back Eddie Robson's plate as Claire was placing the used dishes on the trolley. She thanked him and turned away to scrape the leftovers into a bucket and stack the plate with the rest. For several seconds he didn't move away. She had the feeling that he was regarding her closely, but she didn't look up to find out if she was right. He made her uncomfortable, this big man with his easy assurance and his good looks—and his free-and-easy friends. She wished that Eddie Robson would make a speedy recovery so that they would all leave the island. In some strange way they had disrupted her peace, her newly won serenity.

Chapter Three

The mission owned an ancient Jeep—the only motor vehicle on the island. It was used to convey sick people from other villages to the hospital, and by Father Damien for visiting his scattered parishioners.

When Claire passed by the thatched shed where it was kept, on her way to the hospital on Monday afternoon, she was surprised to see it standing outside, and Father Damien and Scott Carver, both covered in grease, with their heads together under the raised hood.

She hurried inside the building, intent on not being seen, and asked Loretta, who was on clinic duty, what was the matter with the Jeep this time.

'I don't know, but when Father came back from his visiting round this morning it was coughing and wheezing like a mechanical flu victim, and Mr. Carver offered to help. You know how men can't resist trying their hand at fixing an engine gone wrong.'

'For a nun, you sound as though you know a lot about men,' Claire teased, tying her customary white square about her head.

Loretta laughed as she emptied the steriliser with gloved hands. 'I have three brothers. And all of them would be head down under the hood of a car at every opportunity. Actually, I know quite a lot about engines myself. I couldn't help picking it up.'

'Really? I haven't heard you offering to help Father Damien when he's had to fix the Jeep before.'

Loretta dropped a scalpel, made a soft exclamation of annoyance and picked it up deftly. 'Darn it, that will have to be resterilised. Can you see me stripping down an engine in this outfit?'

She looked at her spotless white habit, and Claire laughed. 'Well, hardly,' she admitted.

'Anyway, they don't like help from women,' Loretta said. 'It's a male-brotherhood thing. Women getting in on the act make them feel threatened.'

Smiling, Claire said, 'Do you have sisters as well?'

'Mm. Three. Two are married, the oldest is a nun. That's Cathy; she's a darling. I always wanted to be like her, she was such a serene, confident person. She's quite a lot older than me, and she was always my heroine.'

'And your brothers?'

'One's married and is on Volunteer Service Abroad in Malawi—my little brother. The other two are priests—at least, Tim is, and Peter's in his last year of training.'

Claire looked impressed, and Loretta laughed at her. 'Yes, we're a very religious family. Mum and Dad always said they'd be pleased whatever we did, but they're terribly proud of Tim and Peter. A priest in the family was the pinnacle of Mum's ambition, and she's got two! She's only afraid now of becoming puffed up with the sin of pride.'

'She must be proud of you, too. I'd love to have been part of a big family.'

'It had its moments. We were never very well-off, of course, but then, there was always someone to share your troubles—or good fortune, as the case might be. And we had a lot of fun. Even now we feel close to one another. It's a good preparation for religious life. Some of the novices I trained with found the communal living difficult—they weren't accustomed to it. But I was used to living in a large group, so it was a breeze for me.'

'Had you always wanted to be a nun?' Claire asked.

'More or less. It was either that or be the mother of a large family of my own, I suppose. I was at Cathy's profession, of course, with the family. I thought it was so lovely, seeing her take her final vows. But even before that, her clothing as a novice . . . you know, the candles and flowers and her white bridal gown, and the singing . . . And when we visited her I saw the happiness in her face. . . . She was radiant with it. I knew I could never be as good a person as my sister, but I wanted to try. I decided when I was twelve, and I was lucky, of course, with my family. Some girls find their parents totally opposed to the idea. Mine were just thrilled at the prospect of another vocation in the family. I had every encouragement and was allowed to enter almost straight from school. I would have gone directly from the school to the convent if the order had allowed it, but they insisted on one year "in the world" first.'

'You don't have any regrets?'

'Regrets? No,' Loretta said firmly, pulling off her surgical gloves with decisive movements. 'I'm doing exactly what I've always wanted. What could I ever have regrets about?'

She went to open the door and call in their first patient, but as she pulled it back there was a loud curse from outside and a clang of metal.

The two women looked at each other in surprise, and the half-dozen people waiting in the small anteroom stared towards the outer door.

Sister Loretta took two or three swift steps, but before she reached the outside Father Damien appeared in the doorway with a grim-faced Scott Carver at his elbow.

'Sorry, Loretta,' Father Damien said, 'it looks like I'd better be your first patient today. It seems to be something of an emergency.'

He was holding his left hand elevated and it was dripping blood down his arm and onto the floor.

For a moment Loretta seemed paralysed with surprise. Then she turned, her face rather pale, saying, 'Come in, Father. Claire, we'll need water and disinfectant, of course. And a bandage.'

'Can I do anything?' Scott Carver asked.

'I don't think so,' Claire told him as Loretta followed Father Damien into the clinic. 'Except watch your language, perhaps,' she added rather tartly.

'That,' he answered, 'wasn't me. It was the reverend gentleman himself.'

Her eyes met his amused gaze for a moment, and held. She felt laughter welling up inside her and made her mouth prim. 'Sorry,' she murmured. 'I suppose it was understandable in the circumstances.'

'Very,' he agreed before she firmly closed the door on him.

Father Damien was sitting on a chair while Loretta examined the long, jagged gash in his left hand, starting at the fleshy part of the thumb and ending at the wrist. 'How did you do it?' she asked, sounding severe.

'I'm not exactly sure. The spanner slipped.'

'Well, we'll clean it up first and then have a proper look.'

Claire held the water and disinfectant while the nun bathed the wound, and after a few moments Loretta said, 'It needs stitching. I'll give you a local first and a tetanus shot later.'

She dealt with it in a few minutes with calm efficiency, and Claire helped with the bandaging. Father Damien's tan had hardly altered, and he walked out quite jauntily, his hand in a temporary sling, declaring his intention of supervising the rest of the Jeep repairs.

Claire disposed of the bloodied water and cloths and turned to see Sister Loretta sitting in the chair the priest had vacated, looking pale and leaning forward with a hand to her forehead.

'Loretta!' She went swiftly to the young nun's side. 'Are you ill?'

'I'll be fine in a moment. I'm just . . . Oh!' She put her head down suddenly on her knees, saying in a muffled voice, '. . . just a bit dizzy . . . I expect it's the heat.'

'I'll get Sister Amy,' Claire said.

'*No!*' Loretta's hand shot out to grasp hers, her head going up, then sinking again onto her knees. 'No, please,' she whispered. 'I'll be all right in a minute. It's nothing.'

Claire waited, feeling helpless, then freed her hand to go and get a cloth dunked in cold water. 'Here,' she said, pressing it to the other girl's forehead. 'This may help.'

'Thank you,' Loretta gasped, holding the cloth gratefully against her skin.

Soon she sat up gingerly, her colour returning. 'I'm all right,' she said, handing the cloth back to Claire. 'We'd better be letting our patients in.'

'Are you sure?' Claire asked dubiously.

'It was just a dizzy turn . . . the heat,' Loretta repeated, smiling shakily. 'Nothing, really, Claire. Please don't worry.'

'Has it happened before?'

'Never,' Loretta answered, her voice firmer. 'If it happens again I'll ask Dr. Adams to check me over next time she comes, I promise. It's all right, Claire, honestly. I'm a nurse, remember?'

'You don't want me to mention it,' Claire said shrewdly. It was not a question.

'I'd be grateful if you didn't. It's not worth making a fuss about.' Her eyes pleaded in spite of her casual tone, and Claire said reluctantly, 'Okay, I won't . . . unless it happens again.'

Once more Scott Carver was in the ward when Claire brought in the trolley for the evening meal.

The crewman was showing real improvement now; he had been up and about that day and was able to eat without too much trouble, but when she went in, his employer was sitting by his bed peeling some fruit for him.

He finished what he was doing and came over, taking Eddie's plate from her. But when he had delivered it and seen Eddie take up a fork and start eating without the need for help, he returned to her side.

'He seems much better,' he said, indicating his crewman.

'Yes. You must be glad.' She reached across him for an empty plate.

He forestalled her, picking up two plates from the pile and holding them ready for her to fill. 'Of course. Not that we're eager to leave here.'

'Aren't you?' she said distantly. 'I shouldn't have thought this island was your style at all.'

She replaced the ladle in the pot and made to take the plates from him, but he retained his hold, his eyes faintly surprised and decidedly curious. 'You wouldn't? That sounds as though *you're* pretty eager to *have* us leave.'

'I didn't say that.'

'But you're not denying it, either, I notice . . . Sister. What have we done to get in your hair?' As he said it his eyes shifted to the coiflike headdress she wore, and she fancied she saw derision in them.

She dropped her hands from the plates. 'You and your friends don't belong here,' she said. 'That's all.' She moved to pick another plate from the pile, but he shifted closer to the trolley, preventing her from reaching across without touching him.

'Oh, come on,' he said. 'If we don't belong, neither do you. You people are equally out of place here. What have you really got against us?'

'Nothing,' she said. 'Are you going to take those meals to some patients? Those two beds there.'

She pointed, her voice deliberately imperious, and he met her eyes with an odd spark in his, then turned away without hurry and went to deliver the food as she had directed.

She was relieved to see Sister Martha bustle in as she went to take two more plates over to the beds, but her relief changed to chagrin when Scott Carver said clearly, 'I'll help tonight, Sister, if you have other things to do.'

Sister Martha beamed at him and left, and it was all Claire could do not to glare when she returned to the trolley and found him standing with the ladle in one hand and a plate in the other.

She tightened her lips and took more plates and waited for him to fill them. He spooned food onto one, then hesitated with the ladle poised over the other until she had to look at him, her eyes angry and her cheeks hot.

'What have we done that's so terrible?' he asked softly.

Her patience snapping, she said in a low, unsteady voice, 'You spoil the children with money and teach them to beg while you laugh at them; you patronise the adults and insult their intelligence, and you flaunt your questionable moral standards in their faces! You represent the worst of so-called Western civilisation, and they need you and your kind like they need a hole in the head. So why don't you just up anchor and get out of here and leave us all in peace, Mr. Carver!'

His eyebrows went up, and his lips pursed in a soundless whistle. 'That's quite a mouthful,' he commented.

'You did ask,' she said.

He tipped the ladle to allow the mixture of pork and vegetables to fall onto the empty plate. 'Sure did,' he agreed quietly. 'And got more than I bargained for.' He grinned. 'I always thought nuns were meek-and-mild types. Seems I was mistaken.'

'Have you met Sister Martha?' she asked him.

'Briefly.' Humour lit his eyes, and also speculation. 'I take it she's a tartar. But then, she looks like one. *You* look like . . .'

Her startled eyes flew to his, and he frowned and shook his head. 'No, I guess I shouldn't say that.'

But as she made to turn away he said, 'I think you're mistaken too, though. I resent those accusations of yours.'

Her eyes firmly on the plates of food in her hands, she admitted, 'I shouldn't have said it.'

He filled the plate he held and walked past her with it in his hand. 'You did, though,' he reminded her.

When the meal was over he helped her stack the dishes on the trolley, but this time he followed her as she pushed it through the door, closing it behind them and putting his hand on the trolley to stop her from proceeding to the kitchen.

'Just a word,' he said as she stiffened. He was only inches away. She could feel the warmth emanating from his body, see the beating of a pulse in the tanned hollow of his throat, and the few curling chest hairs revealed by the casually unbuttoned opening of his denim shirt. 'I haven't given any money to the kids on the island,' he told her, 'and I certainly haven't, to my knowledge, patronised or insulted anyone. If my friends have, I'm sorry.' He paused. 'As for our moral standards, aren't you rather jumping to conclusions? I'd like to know what evidence you have for labelling us as the "worst of so-called Western civilisation."'

'I've said I'm sorry,' she muttered, aware that cavorting about almost naked and exchanging kisses, however passionate, in public hardly justified such extreme condemnation.

'No you haven't,' he argued. 'Your words were, "I shouldn't have said that." I don't call that an apology.'

'If it's an apology you want, Mr. Carver, I'll give you one. I'm sorry if I've misjudged you and your friends, and I don't really think you're the *worst* example of modern Western life. Satisfied?'

His breath hissed between his teeth in annoyance. 'You're certainly not my idea of a nun,' he said forcefully.

'Well, I'm sorry about that, too,' she said, trying to sound sweet and humble. 'I don't know what your idea of a nun is, exactly, but fortunately I don't have to conform to it.'

She dared to smile at him then, with a hint of malice behind the deliberate blandness, and was rewarded by seeing a look of angry bafflement on his face. He let go of the trolley and turned abruptly away.

Afterwards she was horrified at herself. She had

let the man get under her skin and ended up trying
to score points off him. It was not only, as he had
pointed out, unsuitable behaviour for a nun or even
an aspiring one, she had an uneasy suspicion that it
was also likely to be dangerous.

'We've been invited to visit the yacht,' Father
Damien told them that evening. 'Scott asked me to
relay the invitation to you all. I think he wasn't quite
sure that it was proper to invite "the ladies," as he
called you. For tonight, anytime after seven, he
said.'

'Are you going?' Sister Amy asked him, looking as
though she wasn't altogether sure herself.

'After this,' he said, indicating his bandaged hand,
'I feel the need of a . . . a medicinal shot of some-
thing stronger than coconut milk. Yes, I'm going.
After dinner.'

'Sister Loretta would have given you a little
brandy, Father, if she'd thought you needed it. We
do keep some in the medicine cabinet.'

Father Damien grinned. 'Don't you approve of my
going, Sister? You can come along to keep an eye on
me.'

'Of course I don't disapprove, Father. For one
thing, it's not my place to judge your actions, and for
another, I'm sure it will do you good to relax for a
little while. But I don't think we'll join you. Sister
Loretta is on duty tonight, and I'm tired. You may
ask Sister Martha if she wants to go, but I doubt it.
And of course Claire must please herself.'

'No, thank you,' Claire said hastily. 'I don't think
I'd enjoy it.'

'You can convey our apologies to Mr. Carver,'

Sister Amy said calmly, 'and thank him for the invitation.'

Father Damien returned later that night with disquieting news. A hurricane warning was out—the yacht's radio had picked it up long after everyone except Sister Loretta, who was on duty, had gone to bed—and the island and its neighbours were right in the path of the storm. Sister Loretta left the ward to warn Sister Amy, and after some consultation it was decided to wake the remainder of the staff and prepare for the worst in case it should happen.

Trying to batten down shutters and secure doors without waking the sleeping patients wasn't easy, but they did the best they could. Then the nuns opened crates in order to have extra medical supplies on hand for emergencies. Claire helped to scout for pieces of timber that could be fastened across windows to save the glass. She hammered in nails while Father Damien held the boards with his good hand. By dawn a stiff breeze was clashing the palm leaves together along the shore, and white water was thundering over the reef and ruffling the usually calm surface of the lagoon. The yacht had been brought about and anchored fore and aft, its sails neatly furled, and several figures could be seen moving about on deck, apparently busy securing everything that could be tied down.

The villagers were astir early, too, looking out with apprehension at the grey sky and shivering in the unaccustomed force of the wind, although it was warm and moist rather than really cold. They scuttled about moving henhouses into sheltered spots and collecting water buckets, dishes, tools and other utensils which normally lay against the walls of the houses or were stacked outside. Some people were strengthening the walls of their homes with extra layers of banana palm thatching and strong liana ropes, and others whose houses had corrugated iron roofs were scrambling over them with hammers in hand, banging down lifting edges and weighting them in some cases with large stones handed up by helpful relatives.

Some of the patients became restless and anxious about their families and their own helplessness, and Claire did her best to help the nuns calm them. To complicate matters further, two women went into labour almost simultaneously, keeping Sister Amy and Sister Loretta busy in the small maternity room. One of them was expected to have twins, and for the other it was her first child.

'I've told everyone they can come to the church and the hospital for shelter,' Father Damien said. The church was the most substantial building on the island, large and built of a kind of concrete made with crushed white coral.

'What about the people on the yacht?' Claire asked him.

'I've offered them the use of the church too. But I'm worried about the two villages on the other side of the island. They must know by now that there's a storm coming, but they've no radio over there and they may not realise how bad it could get. I'd dearly like to drive over and check on their welfare and let them know the church is available to them. But with this hand, I can't manage the Jeep.'

'I'll go,' Claire offered immediately.

He looked harassed. 'I don't think I can let you go on your own, Claire. You've never driven the Jeep, and it's inclined to be temperamental, you know.'

'I've got a licence,' Claire said. 'Show me the gears and I'll do it. We've pretty well done all we can here, haven't we? I know Sister Martha can't drive, and the nursing sisters have their hands full.'

Reluctantly he agreed, and she went to her room for a raincoat, a dark blue cotton scarf to keep the wind from blowing her hair into her eyes as she was driving, and a pair of canvas espadrilles to replace her sandals.

When she came out again she found that the party from the yacht had arrived and were talking to Father Damien. At least, Scott Carver was talking to him, his thumbs hooked into the belt of a pair of denims that had seen better days. Jess leaned with Felix against the side of the Jeep. Sheryl was clinging to Morris' arm, looking rather scared, and the two redheads, Doug and Darlene, were standing to one side together. Darlene was saying, 'Well, I think it's all rather exciting. I've never actually been in a hurricane before.'

Claire couldn't help casting her a withering glance as she climbed into the driver's seat of the Jeep, tossing her raincoat in the back. The islanders, who stood to lose their homes and crops if the storm was a really bad one, wouldn't think of it as exciting.

She saw Scott Carver turn and stare appraisingly at her dark-coloured scarf, then rapidly run his eyes over her pale blue button-through dress and down her bare legs to the navy espadrilles.

Father Damien excused himself and came over to show her the gears. She wished the seat would shift forward to allow her better access to the pedals. She could reach them, but not comfortably. She also wished that the small audience would go away, but they were all watching, although Felix and Jess had moved and were now a few feet away from the vehicle. Scott Carver, on the other hand, had moved closer.

'Where's she going?' he demanded, frowning.

Father Damien explained, and the other man looked at Claire. 'Have you driven this thing before?'

'I'll manage,' she said briefly.

He turned to Father Damien and said, 'I told you we'd help in any way we could. I'll go.' Turning his eyes back to Claire, he said, 'Get down.'

'You don't know the way,' she protested.

His eyebrows went up. 'How big is the island? Ten miles across? Less?'

'That isn't the point,' she told him. 'You can't just go as the crow flies, barging through banana plantations and taro patches.' The road, in fact, almost skirted the island, meandering inland to avoid difficult patches of coastal trees and branching off amid scattered gardens and plantations.

'Okay, so you can show me the way,' he said, putting a foot on the running board. 'Move over.'

She looked helplessly at Father Damien, but he appeared to be relieved, if anything. 'Thank you,' he said. 'That's by far the best idea, Claire.'

Reluctantly she shifted to the other side of the bench seat.

Scott Carver didn't waste any time; he had the engine going and the Jeep backing away from the hospital compound in about two seconds flat.

'Right,' he said crisply. 'Which way?'

She directed him, and soon they were roaring along the narrow track which barely allowed room for the Jeep's wheels to pass between the tree trunks. Overhanging greenery brushed its tattered canopy as they passed.

The wind was rising all the time, but the humidity still kept the air warm and sticky once they left the sea behind. The Jeep slowed as they came to another pathway, and Claire indicated a right turn.

Picking up speed again, her companion glanced at her and asked, 'How long have you been on the island?'

'Almost eleven months.'

He gave her another look, interested and curious. 'Did you volunteer, or were you sent?'

'I volunteered.'

'For how long?'

'A year.'

'So your time's nearly up?'

'Yes.'

He slowed to negotiate a section of rough, rutted track, and said carefully, 'Will you be sorry to leave?'

'Yes.'

His mouth twisted wryly. 'You haven't taken a vow of silence, have you?'

'No.'

His breath whistled between his teeth in exasperation. 'Just trying to make conversation, Sister.'

'I'm sorry,' she murmured.

'What?' He hadn't heard her over the noise of the engine.

She turned to him and said loudly, 'I'm sorry I'm not entertaining enough for you.'

She wasn't prepared for the sudden stop he made, and had to clutch at the dashboard in front of her.

She looked at him, bewildered and somewhat apprehensive, and saw that he was staring straight ahead through the dusty windscreen, his mouth grim. Finally he turned and faced her, his eyes alight with barely controlled temper, and said in a level voice, 'Look, I know you don't like me—I'm not sure why, except that you seem to have projected a whole lot of narrow-minded prejudices onto me, and if you weren't . . . what you are, I'd be tempted to do something about that, maybe something quite drastic. But in spite of your low opinion of me, I do have some principles left. Anyway, it looks like we're stuck with each other for the next couple of hours. I thought we could at least have a normal, casual conversation—unless that's against your rules or something? Is it a sin for you to speak to a man?'

Dumbly Claire shook her head.

He shrugged. 'I guess you're just not used to talking to men. How long have you been . . . ?'

Claire felt a flicker of embarrassed apprehension cross her face.

He noticed it and sighed. 'That's another personal question, I suppose, that you won't want to answer. If you prefer to spend the time in total silence, okay. Just let me know. I like to know where I stand, that's all.'

He was waiting for her answer, his hands tight on the wheel, his eyes direct and hard.

Claire found her voice at last. 'I didn't mean to be rude, Mr. Carver,' she said huskily. 'I suppose I'm just not used to men of your type.' She saw his lips tighten rather ominously at that and hurried on. 'I mean, I think you're perfectly right—about having a normal, casual conversation. I was worrying about the islanders, that's all. Don't you think we should be getting on?'

'We've lost all of thirty seconds,' he said rather mockingly, but he started the engine again and they began to move.

He didn't try to begin another conversation, and after a few uncomfortable minutes she said, 'I'd have thought you'd need more than one crewman for your yacht. It's quite a big craft.'

He threw her a glance, then grinned faintly, as though giving her points for trying. 'It's a seventy-footer. The other men help. That's why I brought them along. Doug has some racing experience, and Felix and Morris are quite useful on a boat. And Jess is always willing to have a go, though she's only sailed small craft before.'

'Oh, then they're crew—not just guests.'

'A bit of both. Darlene and Sheryl, though, are purely decorative.' He shot her a sardonic look as though daring her to comment.

'Who decided to sail her through the reef?' she asked.

'I did, of course. We could have used the motor, but . . .' He shrugged. '. . . it was more interesting sailing her in.'

She looked at him covertly, wondering if he had been showing off or had simply enjoyed the excitement of a tricky manoeuvre under sail. She said,

'Father Damien told us you once went exploring in the New Guinea Highlands.'

'That's right. Which way here?'

She directed him through the fork that they were approaching, and they drove on through the banana plantations.

He said, 'I was in New Guinea two years ago. Ever been there?'

She shook her head, and he began to tell her something about the country and the Stone Age tribes he had visited. When he stopped she was so intrigued that she began questioning him eagerly for more information. 'How did you manage to get onto the team?' she asked him.

'I financed the expedition.'

'I see.' With money, of course, almost anything was possible. He had just decided to explore New Guinea and set up an expedition to do it, handpicked by himself.

'No,' he said, reading her face. 'It wasn't quite like that. A bloke I went to university with is an anthropologist. He suggested I put up some money for the expedition, and I asked to be taken along. He knew I was physically fit enough, so he let me be the dogsbody and cook.'

'Cook?'

He slanted her a grin. 'I can cook. In any case, they weren't too fussy, and most of the food came out of tins and packets.'

'What did you study at university?'

'Economics. That was my father's idea.'

'You mean, you didn't want to?'

He grinned. 'All I wanted was to swan around the world, see as much of it as I could—especially the parts not too many people had seen. Like the islands of the Pacific. My father had already made more money than I was ever going to need. I couldn't see the point of spending four years of my life learning how to make more. My father didn't see it that way. I went to university to please him. I passed the exams, then I persuaded him to invest in racing cars and take me on as a driver. At least it was productive in its way, and I managed to convince him I was doing something useful for the firm. The publicity was good, and that had some influence with him. And it involved some travelling, though not the sort I would have preferred. Anyway, I managed to keep away from an office desk for a few more years. I'd only have been some sort of figurehead in the firm. Then I started yachting. He wasn't keen on ocean racing, but he did appreciate that it involved skill and competition. He was very competitive himself, so he went along with that, too, in the end. Of course, another way of looking at it is that he simply spoiled me rotten.'

'He must have been very fond of you,' she said, rather wistfully.

'I suppose he was. Parents tend to be that way about their kids. I was fond of him, too.' His voice, in spite of his throwaway air, deepened a little with the admission.

'But not enough to do what he wanted?' Her own voice had hardened a little, and she realised with a twinge of shame that she was envious.

He looked at her curiously. 'He didn't push it too hard. I guess, although he had tried to train me up to take his place, the truth is that he didn't really want to hand over the reins. As long as I turned up every so often and reported in for a month or two he was reasonably happy. Even after he died, the corporation he'd built up was so well organised that it was able to run quite adequately without me. That's when I went on those expeditions. By comparison, this is a holiday cruise. It's also what I've always wanted to do, though, sail round the Pacific on my own boat.'

'So now you're fulfilling your ambition,' she commented.

'Yeah.'

He sounded wearily sarcastic, and she said, 'Hasn't it lived up to your expectations?'

He shrugged almost impatiently. 'I guess nothing that you've looked forward to for so long lives up to expectations.'

They reached the first village sooner than she had anticipated. Their warning and the offer of shelter at the church were received philosophically. As much as possible, the people were preparing for a big blow, but looking about at the flimsy huts and the inadequate protection of the slim palms surrounding them, Claire felt a terrifying sense of helplessness. She offered transport in the Jeep to anyone old or infirm who wished to take advantage of Father Damien's suggestion and come with them to the church, but although one or two families urged a frail grandmother or pregnant mother to accept, no one would leave their loved ones, and in the second village it was exactly the same.

'We'll come back as soon as it's over in case you need help,' she promised them, climbing back into the Jeep, her skirt whipping about her knees and the scarf fluttering like a flag in the growing strength of the wind.

'Is that all we can do?' Scott Carver asked, apparently sharing her sense of futility.

'I'm afraid so,' she sighed. 'It's not much, is it?'

'No, it's not much.' He drummed his fingers on the wheel, surveyed the rapidly darkening sky and said abruptly, 'Well, we'd better be heading back, then. We don't want to get caught in it.'

He drove fast, with a growing sense of urgency as the palms began bending and swaying about them, the stiff leaves clacking ominously, and bits of branches went whirling away in the wind. They must have covered more than half the distance when the engine suddenly coughed and died.

'*Hell!*' he exclaimed, and then glanced at Claire, muttering between his teeth, 'Sorry.'

'It's all right,' she assured him.

Already swinging himself down to the ground, he paused and grinned at her. 'Understandable in the circumstances?'

Claire smiled back, recognising her own words. 'Very.'

He laughed out loud and went to raise the hood.

Claire, too, got down to have a look. Not that there was much she could do. 'What is it?' she asked.

'Will you understand if I tell you?'

'Probably not,' she had to admit.

'Then I won't waste time explaining. Get back in and try the starter for me, will you?'

She tried, and tried again, while he fiddled, swore softly to himself, and fiddled again.

Eventually he slammed the hood down and came

back to her. 'It isn't going anywhere today,' he told her. 'Do you think you can walk from here?'

'Yes. We can take shortcuts because we don't have to stick to the vehicle tracks. It's only a few miles.'

The light had turned eerily yellow, and the palms overhead thrashed about angrily below a sky that was suddenly leaden. He looked up at it and said, 'I just hope we can make it. Come on.'

Chapter Four

$\mathcal{T}$he engine noise of the Jeep had drowned the sound of the wind, but now it was all about them, a whistling moan that gradually increased in intensity. Claire reached into the Jeep for her coat, but as she lifted it the wind caught it, snatching it from her fingers and hurling it high into the air to disappear among the trees.

Scott bit out an impatient exclamation, making a futile grab as it flew past him, and Claire watched in dismay. 'Never mind,' she said. 'It doesn't matter.'

He shrugged. 'Nothing to be done about it, anyway, is there? Let's go.'

The wind made them stagger as they headed down the primitive road in the direction of the mission, and the ends of Claire's scarf stung her cheek. Her eyes watered, and she grimly put her head down and kept her feet moving in spite of the increasing force of the gale. A few heavy drops of rain plummeted through the palms, plopping onto the dusty ground and making tiny sandspurts. One or two hit Claire's face, and she flinched. A couple of cold drops struck her shoulders and seeped into her dress.

They stuck to the same track for a while; then Claire recognised a footpath that would cut off some distance and motioned to Scott that they should take it. But they had been following it for only about ten minutes when the wind suddenly seemed to stop. Claire halted abruptly, instinctively looking up, and the man beside her put his hand on her arm, unconsciously gripping hard.

'I think this is it,' he muttered, lifting his head to survey the unnaturally still tops of the trees surrounding them.

Claire held her breath. The silence was total, except for the distant boom of the waves on the reef. Even the birds were quiet. Then the wind returned in full force, tearing the tops off the palms and snatching them away, roaring and howling like a savage animal on the rampage, and rain hurled itself from the heavens as though a giant bucket had been overturned.

Claire's scarf was ripped from her head, and the wind buffeted her until she reeled, only the hard hand on her arm keeping her upright as she gasped with sheer fright.

'Come on!' he shouted, and pulled her along the now barely visible path as their shoes filled with water. They were both soaked in the first few seconds, and her hair was plastered to her head, her dress clinging about her thighs, impeding her legs as she stumbled along beside him.

A palm tree in front of them suddenly leaned more than the others, its roots freeing themselves, and as it lifted and crashed Scott pushed Claire aside and onto the ground, coming after her and sheltering her with his body half beside and half on top of her.

He raised his head and tried to wipe moisture from his eyes, looking about them in a kind of desperation. She saw him say something to her as she sat up, trying to get back on her feet, but had to shake her head, not understanding what he said, the noise of the rain and the wind deafening her.

He pulled her closer, his hands on her shoulders, and shouted, *'Is there any shelter around here?'*

She shook her head, knowing that they were too far from any habitation to make it in this. Despairingly she looked about, and then looked again. There was a clearing here, a bend in the path around the trunk of a breadfruit tree with an oddly shaped, malformed branch. It looked familiar.

Swaying on her feet, she tried to clear her eyes and her brain, to think in spite of the noise and the pelting rain and the fear that she couldn't quell. He was standing too, holding on to a nearby palm trunk, his arm hooked about its ridged surface, his other arm firmly round her waist. She was grateful for the support.

Hope began to stir, and she leaned close to him, her hand on his wet shirt, willing him to listen.

He bent his head, and she put her lips close to his ear. 'I think I can find some shelter!'

He nodded and shouted, *'Lead me to it!'*

She took a deep breath and indicated the way they should go. She only hoped that she was right. The storm disoriented her, but she gained confidence as she glimpsed other familiar landmarks through the driving rain.

He followed her lead, his arm about her waist steadying her as she faltered against the wind. And then, at last, there it was—the clump of old twisted trunks that formed the 'secret house' that Munda and Tana had made their own.

Well, she thought, they wouldn't mind her using it, and she didn't suppose in the circumstances that she was bound by her promise not to tell anyone about it.

'Up there!' She pointed. 'We have to climb.'

Again he nodded, apparently understanding, and helped her to negotiate the smooth curves of the intertwined trunks, slippery now with the rain. One piece of peeling bark caught at her dress and snagged it, but she pulled free and reached the dark cavelike hollow, exhausted but safe.

She fell through the entrance, huddling as far into the recess as she could, and he followed, darkening the entrance even further for an instant before he joined her, panting and laughing, and pushing wet hair away from his eyes.

'Whew! Thank G—Thank goodness you found this,' he said. 'I think it might have saved our lives.'

Stifling an urge to giggle, Claire said primly, 'I think it would be quite in order to thank God, Mr. Carver. I intend to.'

Becoming accustomed to the dimness, she could see the appreciative grin that he gave her. 'You do that,' he said tolerantly. 'And in the circumstances, I think it would be quite in order for you to call me Scott, don't you?'

She didn't answer.

After a few moments, looking about and noting the mats and the carved canoe and decorative shells, he said, 'What is this place, anyway?'

'Some of the children play here. They showed it to me just a few days ago when I nearly discovered them by accident. I'm not supposed to tell anyone, but I think they'll forgive me.'

'They'd better.' He paused. 'Are you okay?'

'Yes, thank you. Wet, but otherwise fine. And you?'

'Much the same. I think we've been lucky, all things considered. That storm out there is a real stinker.'

'Yes. I hope the islanders can survive it.' Their voices sounded strange, enclosed in their small shell of relative quiet while outside they could still hear the full fury of the storm.

'No use worrying about it,' he said. 'We'll find out when it's all over. You did pretty well out there.'

'For a woman?' she suggested dryly.

'I didn't actually mean that.' He paused, eyeing her with speculation. 'Are nuns allowed to be feminists?'

'Quite a few of them are,' she said carefully. 'Of course, not everyone approves.'

'Well, for the record, Sister, I approve of you. You're one in a million.'

The praise warmed her incredibly. She had to take a moment to steady her voice before she said, 'Thank you. You were rather useful, too.'

He laughed softly. 'For a playboy?'

She asked slowly, 'Are you a playboy?'

He stretched out beside her, leaning on one elbow. 'I had the impression that you think so. Of course, I've always had money, and certainly I've done a fair amount of . . . playing about on the strength of it. As I told you, since my father died, and even before, I've done just what I wanted, more or less. If I want to see New Guinea or the Amazon, I can. If I feel like playing the tables at Monte or Vegas, I do it. Not that I enjoy gambling much. Maybe that's a pity. I could have gambled away my fortune and had to start again from scratch. That'd be a challenge, wouldn't it?'

'Is a challenge what you want from life, Mr. Carver?'

'I thought you were going to call me Scott.'

She didn't reply, and he said, answering her question, 'It's better than boredom.'

'Do you get bored easily?' she asked him, irony in her voice.

'It's an occupational hazard of the wealthy,' he answered, matching her tone with mockery of his own. 'Don't you know that?'

'Did you ever read the Bible, Mr. Carver?'

'Parts of it. Are you going to quote it at me?'

'I just wondered if you know the story of the rich young man.'

'Yes, as a matter of fact. He wanted to know how to win eternal life, and Jesus said to him, "Sell all you have and follow me." The trouble is, I don't believe in eternal life.'

'That's a pity,' Claire said softly. 'For an unbeliever, this life must be very empty. No wonder you're bored.'

'Not at all. I said it's an occupational hazard, but I make sure my life is very full.'

'Of what?' she challenged him.

'Wine, women and song, of course. That's the answer you've got on your mind, isn't it?'

'What's *your* answer?'

'Adventure, risk, challenge.'

'Why?'

'Why?' he repeated. 'I don't know. Perhaps because I had a pampered childhood. I used to fantasise about what it would be like to be poor.'

Claire laughed softly. 'A reversal of the usual childhood fantasy.'

'So I suppose.'

'You've never dared to make the fantasy real, though.'

'No. Oh, I've done my small bit for charity in various ways, because I've seen real poverty in my travels, and if it interests you, it makes me feel guilty . . . guilty but hopeless. It's all a drop in the bucket. If I gave away all that I have, it wouldn't really make any difference in the long run. Perhaps that's just an excuse for a basically selfish point of view.'

'I'm not judging you,' she said softly. 'I'm sorry if I seemed to, before. . . .'

He put out a hand and closed it over hers as it lay in her lap. Claire stiffened and took her hand away, and for a moment the small, narrow space where they were confined seemed filled with tension.

Then he moved abruptly, sitting up. She had the distinct impression that he was angry, but his voice was calm as he said casually, 'Don't you think that you and your . . . colleagues are doing more to corrupt the natives than my friends and I?'

'Corrupt?' Her head went up indignantly.

'You're certainly more bent on eradicating the island traditions than any casual visitors could ever be. You want to replace their religion, their medicine, their educational system, with "Western Christianity." It's a deliberate policy with you, so aren't you just as culpable, if not more so, than we are?'

'We don't see it like that. . . .'

'No,' he said derisively, 'I don't suppose you would. Do-gooders have a tendency to see things in terms of black and white.'

Rallying, she said firmly, 'I think that's unfair. It's true we hope to convert the islanders to our faith, but we don't force them, and we don't denigrate their traditions. Of course, I know that earlier missionaries were sometimes too zealous and that they destroyed cultural values and some tangible cultural symbols—carvings and that sort of thing— that perhaps could have been preserved.'

'Or should have.'

'Or should have,' Claire acknowledged. 'Though it's easy for us to criticise now, not having to endure the conditions that they did, or cope with cannibalism and the kind of horrors that were common then. But we don't work like that now. We try to separate the Christian elements from the purely cultural aspects of our own society, and not to impose our own social and cultural values on other peoples. We have a message to spread, but we're aware that the Gospel of Christ is for all people, and that each community is entitled to its own ways of worship within the wider community of the church as a whole.'

He raised his brows skeptically. 'You are? The hymns I heard the other day sounded remarkably familiar . . . from my younger days when I attended Sunday school back in Brisbane.'

'Perhaps they did, but they were sung in the language of the island. And Father Damien is encouraging the people to compose their own songs in traditional style, to be used in church.'

'Really? It still seems to me like grafting one culture onto another.'

'No . . . it's grafting some fresh insights and new ideas onto the old culture . . . but the old culture, the island way of life, is the tree; the new religion is a young, vigorous slip that will grow into a strong branch and become a part of the tree like the other branches, in time.'

He laughed and inclined his head. 'That's neat. And clever.'

Encouraged, she went in to attack. 'You're not going to say that the islanders should have been left in ignorance of modern medical techniques, are you? Do you know what the death rate was, especially among the children, before the mission was set up here in the thirties?'

'Okay, tell me.'

She told him, and told him how the teaching of hygiene and elementary first aid had helped to lower the rate of disease and death, and how education would be essential soon, for the advent of 'progress' in the form of modern amenities and more contact with the rest of the world was unavoidable, and the population was growing at such a rate that within a few years some of the islanders would be forced to leave, while the remainder would need to adopt more efficient farming methods and possibly participate in more trade, in order to survive.

'Your fault,' he suggested. 'If you hadn't halved the death rate, the population would have remained pretty stable.'

Her eyes flashing, Claire said, 'That's a dreadfully callous way of looking at it. They're your fellow human beings!'

'I'm not denying it. Just pointing out that when outsiders come in and solve a problem, they're apt to create a whole lot more.'

'Is that your considered opinion?'

'That's a fact, and you can't deny it.'

'All right,' she conceded, 'I won't deny it. It seems to me it's a lesser problem, though. Death is very final. The other problems . . . We have time to solve those.'

'What are you doing about the birth rate?' he asked bluntly, a slightly malevolent gleam in his eyes. 'Your church doesn't tolerate curbing it, isn't that so?'

'Not entirely,' Claire said carefully. 'Sister Amy and Sister Loretta teach the women natural methods of regulating births. They're harmless, without side effects, easily learnt by people who are accustomed to observing natural phenomena and very effective when properly used.'

'You got that from a textbook!' he accused her.

Claire laughed. 'No, from Sister Amy.'

He grinned. 'Well, you wouldn't have any first-hand knowledge yourself.'

Colouring faintly, she looked away. 'No.'

His mouth went wry. 'Sorry.'

'No, it's all right.' She smiled slightly and glanced at him.

He looked at the opening to their haven as a gust of wind slipped inside, making them shiver. 'I suppose this could last for hours.'

'I suppose it could,' she agreed. Their snug shelter muted the storm's fury, but outside it still raged unabated. Now and then, as if to remind them, the wind threw a handful of twigs and leaves and a flurry of rain in through the narrow opening, and a cold little draught stirred the air. For a long time they sat in silence, while the wind grew stronger and reached a pitch of noise that would have made conversation impossible even in the cave. Then it gradually sank to a muted howl, and the sounds of falling trees and the surf crashing on the shore penetrated to their shelter. Scott went to the entrance, unable to stand up straight, and looked out for a while. When he came back Claire was still sitting where he had left her. She was beginning to feel chilled, the soaked clothing that clung to her body getting colder by the minute.

'What sort of childhood did you have?' he asked her suddenly, hunching his shoulders up against the smooth bark behind him, raising one knee and stretching out the other leg in front of him.

'Not like yours,' she said. 'I was an orphan.' Sort of, an inner voice added. She didn't want to tell him her life story.

But he was saying, 'Really? A genuine, honest-to-goodness orphan?'

For a moment she was silent. Then she said coolly, 'No. Not really. I had a mother. She found a rich husband for herself and didn't want me cluttering up her new life.'

'I see,' he said. 'I didn't mean to be flippant. Sounds like you had a rough time.'

'Oh, I was very sorry for myself for a long time,' she answered. 'But I'm quite happy now.'

'Are you? Happy . . . or just content?'

'Is there a difference?'

'I think so.'

She moved restlessly. 'Then I suppose I'm both.'

'Suppose?' he repeated. He regarded her thoughtfully for a few moments. 'I don't understand you . . . your way of life. You know that, don't you?'

'I know. It's hard to explain it to . . . to someone like you.'

'Try me?' he invited her. 'Tell me why a beautiful, spirited girl wants to shut herself away in a convent.'

'It's really very simple. I want to dedicate my life to others and, through them, to God.'

'I still don't understand.'

'No. I don't expect you to.'

He picked up a tiny shell that lay on the mat close to his hand and tossed it in the air a few times, catching it again in long, lean fingers. Then he closed his fist on it and said, 'You know, sometimes, out on the ocean at night, when there's nothing but me and the boat and the sea and the stars . . . I get the strangest feeling. I can't describe it in any way, except that it's a sense of being watched over, being . . . communicated with. That's the closest I've come to believing in your God.'

He tossed the shell once more, then lofted it into the darkness near the doorway.

When he looked back at her his eyes glittered with

laughter. His mouth twisted. 'If my friends could see me now . . . What a position to be in. Stranded in the middle of a tropical cyclone—with a nun!' He raised his eyes heavenwards and shook his head, his soft laughter echoing round the small chamber.

Claire smiled. 'What's the difference between being stranded with a nun and being stranded with anyone else?'

The laughter stopped as he looked at her, though a smile still lingered about his mouth. 'The difference,' he drawled, 'is that if you'd been Darlene or Sheryl or Jess, believe me, we wouldn't be sitting around discussing theology and life-styles!'

A flood of extraordinary sensation flowed through her like a tidal wave. She met his teasing eyes and knew exactly what he meant, and her mind flashed pictures of him and Jess lying on the floor of the shelter as Jess had lain on the beach with Felix, uninhibitedly kissing, of Darlene offering him the suntan lotion, of him anointing her back with it. And shockingly, unbelievably, she was shaken by a fierce, totally consuming desire for him to touch her, kiss her, make love to her as he would have to any of those other women if they had been alone there with him.

For the first time in her life she was overwhelmed by sexual desire, and it terrified her. She saw his smile fade and his eyes narrow in stunned shock, and knew that he had seen her unguarded expression and understood it.

Shamed and horrified, she wrenched her gaze away from him and raised a hand to hide her hot face. Shakenly she said, 'You mean . . . any one of them? I've never . . . quite understood the . . . the relationships between all of you.'

'I doubt if you could,' he said sardonically. 'Except that Darlene and Doug are twins . . . brother and sister.'

'Oh!' That did surprise her. 'I hadn't thought of that.'

'What did you think of, I wonder?' he murmured. 'Orgies and partner-swapping?'

'No, of course not!' She took her hand away to look at him indignantly, but he was regarding her with eyes that were too sharply questioning and aware, and she quickly looked away again. 'But you must admit that what you've just said suggests . . . suggests a certain . . . freedom.'

'That's the name of the game,' he said carelessly. 'No one was heavily committed to anyone. I thought we'd be able to keep it light that way. No jealousies and playing off one person against another. Of course, there should have been another lady, but she got seasick and asked to be let off at Tahiti. Felix hasn't gone anywhere without a pretty girl in tow for years, and this time it was Sheryl, but he got bored with her and developed a yen for Jess. Jess is her own woman, always has been, we've been friends and occasional lovers for years. She's what's known as a good sort. Doug asked if he could bring his sister . . . it seemed a good idea at the time. But Darlene's a natural femme fatale, trying to play Morris off against me. If she's wise she'll settle for him. I'm tired of her games, and she sure isn't going to wangle a wedding ring out of me, which I guess is what she has in mind.'

'It sounds highly complicated.'

'Not really.'

'You think any of them would have been ready to . . .' She broke off, wishing she hadn't started that sentence.

He looked at her almost pityingly, then shrugged. 'If Darlene had been here with me, she'd be making a play in a big way, and I don't flatter myself that it's just my beautiful body she's after. She and Doug like to hang about the fringe of the jet set, but they've very little money of their own. Jess would have treated it all as a lark, and been willing to while away the time with a little light lovemaking. And Sheryl, being a woman slightly scorned, is just dying to find someone to help her make Felix sit up and take notice of her again. And I guess I'd do as well as the next man.'

And if he didn't think I was a nun, she thought, *I'd do as well as the next woman.*

Aloud she said, 'You don't really care about any of them, do you?'

'Not much. I'll tell you something—spending a lot of time in a confined space with people soon reveals an awful lot about their characters. You can be friends with someone for years and yet learn more in a few days on a boat than you've ever known. And a lot that you never wanted to know.'

'I saw a movie once about a submarine that went down to the bottom and couldn't be raised,' she said. 'It was saying the same thing.'

He grinned. 'Preserve me,' he said, 'from being caught in a downed submarine with Darlene.'

She couldn't help it, she giggled. Like a schoolgirl,

her hand over her mouth, shoulders shaking with mirth.

When she stopped, her eyes filled with tears of laughter, and looked at him, he was smiling openly, and the atmosphere seemed to have lightened visibly.

'You shouldn't say things like that,' she told him, trying to be serious. 'It's not kind.'

He grimaced at her. 'I don't have to be kind. That's *your* mission in life, not mine.'

'Hedonist!' she said feebly.

'I admit it. Sure I couldn't persuade you to join me in that?'

His look was half-amused, half-speculative, and she closed her lips on a smile, trying to be distant. 'I'm not the type.'

He laughed and said, 'I don't suppose you've any idea how seductive that is!'

Seductive! Intrigued and alarmed, she couldn't help demanding as her eyes flew to his, 'What is?'

'The way you prim up your mouth when it's trying to smile after you've said something you think you shouldn't—or when I have.'

'Oh!'

'It doesn't work, you know. All it does is make your mouth look deliciously kissable.'

She gasped and flushed, and he said wryly, 'Must I apologise again? I suppose that remark was out of line too.'

In muffled tones she said, 'Yes, it was, rather. I realise you didn't mean it.'

'Who told you that?' he asked with sudden cynicism, and she said, 'I know it's difficult for you, being alone with a woman you can't . . . flirt with, but please don't!'

There was a short silence. Then he said soberly, 'Okay. I don't mean to embarrass you, believe me.'

He got up and went again to the entrance, staying there for some time.

The conversation had taken her mind off her cold, wet clothes, but now she began to feel the discomfort acutely. She hugged her arms about herself and huddled into the corner, shivering.

'It's still pelting down out there,' he said, coming back to hunker down close by. 'I think the wind might be dropping slightly, but I wouldn't care to take a bet on that, either. We could be stuck here for quite a while.'

Involuntarily she gave a little whimper of distress, just a small sound, but he peered at her in the gloom and said, 'Are you okay?'

Claire nodded. If she spoke, her teeth would chatter, so she kept them tightly closed.

He frowned and leaned closer. 'You're shivering! Are you cold?'

'Aren't . . . you?' she managed to whisper.

He touched her hand with his fingers. 'Not like that! You're frozen. Come here!'

He reached for her and pulled her into his arms, and after a moment of rigid resistance she gave in and snuggled against him. There was nothing at all sexual in the embrace; he only wanted to warm her, and she had a desperate need to be warm.

It was bliss to feel him near her, the heat emanating from his body dispelling the awful chill. His arms were strong and comforting, and he began rocking her gently, almost as though she were a baby. Her teeth stopped chattering, and she sighed and relaxed completely, her eyes half-closed, her cheek against his shirt that had almost dried on him. He moved a hand and began to caress her hair, his fingers stroking the short, damp curls.

His thumb skimmed over the outline of her ear, and she was suddenly conscious of the hard, regular rhythm of his heart under her palm. She felt his breath against the smooth skin of her temple. He murmured something, moving his head slightly, and his fingers brushed lightly across her back. She inhaled the musky male scent of his skin along with the smell of rain and damp cloth.

A faint shudder ran through her, and his arms instinctively tightened, holding her closer. She had begun to shiver again, uncontrollably, but not with cold. Warmth was spreading inside her, suffusing her body with a delicious fever, and yet she could not stop trembling.

She heard him murmur again, caught the word 'Honey . . .' and then 'Don't . . .'

'I'm all right,' she said in a strangled whisper, making a feeble attempt to move away from him, but his arms didn't slacken. 'Please . . . let me go.'

Even as she said it, she stopped struggling and lay against him, as though exhausted. She clenched her hands against his chest, trying to summon the strength to pull away, to stop her ridiculous trembling, and heard him draw a sharp breath.

His hand came under her chin and raised her face with almost brutal suddenness to his. His eyes blazed, catching her expression before she could veil its naked longing or hide the desire in her eyes.

She saw his lips move in a soundless exclamation,

and then his mouth was on hers, taking it with the sweet violence of passion, sending her spinning into a hurricane of emotion that blacked out thought. His lips were cool at first, and then warm and soft before they hardened with sensual demand. The contours of his mouth shaped hers, until her lips parted involuntarily and she found herself clinging drowningly to his shoulders, unable to deny him the response that he had unlocked with the first touch. His hands roved over her back and into her hair, turning her head to a new angle to allow him to coax her mouth farther open and let him explore it deeply with his tongue, an intimate exploration that went on and on until she was dizzy with pleasure and on fire with a terrible craving for more.

They were locked together, swaying in each other's arms, the storm outside forgotten completely in the storm of this unexpected, totally absorbing kiss.

He changed his position slightly and lifted her so that she lay across his lap. She heard herself as if from a great distance give a small moan as his lips at last lifted from hers, and her hands sought unsteadily for his face, his head, tangled in his damp hair and blindly returned his mouth to hers.

He growled softly deep in his throat, and his hand found her breast, closing over the swelling curve and making her shudder with drowsy sensation. His mouth left hers and he buried his lips at the base of her throat, and she gave a long, hoarse sigh of pleasure as her head fell back, her body tautly arched under his hands and his mouth.

Then, suddenly, cold, wet droplets of rain fell on her face, and something brushed scratchily against her cheek, so that she opened startled eyes, shocked back to reality. Her head was almost at the entrance, and the rain and a handful of leaves had been blown into the shelter, breaking into her sensual trance.

In half a second she realised the appalling, unbelievable thing that she was doing and jackknifed in unthinking reaction, so that his arms fell away in surprise.

'No!' she cried thinly, twisting away from him, scurrying instinctively towards the opening and out into the storm.

The rain blinded her and the wind flattened her against the tree as she scrambled to the ground, her dress riding up to her thighs, catching on a piece of peeling bark, the buttons tearing from the material. She half-slithered and half-fell to the base of the tree, slivers of loose bark scratching stingingly at her bared legs, and landed on her knees, struggling to her feet only to be hurled against the tree trunk by the force of the gale.

She vaguely heard Scott shouting, and when he appeared beside her she started and tried to run, only to be spun back against his hard chest by his hand on her arm.

She struggled, sobbing, until he shook her roughly, and in spite of the noise of the storm she heard him yelling, *'Stop it, you little fool! You can't go anywhere in this. You've got to come back!'*

It was true, and she took hold of herself with an effort, biting her lower lip until it hurt, then nodded defeatedly.

He helped her to climb back into the hollow, and she retreated to the far corner and huddled there miserably, panting and trying to cover her thighs with the parted halves of her skirt.

'What have you done to yourself, you idiot?' he said roughly, coming over to her and looking, appalled, at the blood slowly staining her skirt.

'They're only scratches,' she said. 'They'll need a bit of disinfectant—when we get back.'

He put out a hand to pull back her skirt, and she flinched away from him.

His mouth went grim, and his eyes caught hers and held them with an angry gaze. 'I'm not going to rape you,' he said. 'Let me see how bad they are.'

She shook her head. 'You can't do anything to help,' she said.

For answer he simply caught both her hands, transferring them in an unbreakable grip to one of his, and twitched back her skirt, ignoring her efforts to stop him.

She sat still then, while he took a good long look. Then he carefully replaced her skirt, let her go and began to strip off his shirt.

He met her startled eyes for a moment, smiled grimly and, holding the shirt in both hands, began tearing it up.

'Don't!' she said.

'Why? Is the sight of my manly chest driving you wild?'

She flushed and averted her eyes, a choking sensation in her own chest preventing her from making any answer even if she could have thought of one.

'Don't I wish . . .' he said softly, and then moved away, going briefly outside and returning with two pieces of dripping-wet fabric in his hands.

Knowing that protest would be useless, she let him push back her skirt again and bathe the blood away, revealing the long, raised weals. His touch was very gentle.

'You shouldn't have come after me,' she said jerkily. 'Your clothes were nearly dry before.'

'And they'll dry again,' he said. 'What's left of them.'

He didn't have much left, only his jeans, now that he had ruined his shirt for her sake. She looked down at the strong hands that could be so tender as they pressed the damp cloth against her flesh, then looked away again.

'What happened before . . .' he said, his eyes intent on what he was doing. 'I'm sorry if it upset you. I suppose it's a mortal sin or something.'

Her voice muffled, she managed to say, 'No . . . not quite.'

She thought he was laughing silently. For a minute his hands stopped their careful ministrations. Then he said, 'I see.' After a moment he added, 'I didn't plan it, you know.'

'I know,' she said in a low voice. 'It was my fault.'

With one hand holding the cloth against her leg, he lifted the other and brushed her cheek with the backs of his fingers. 'Took yourself by surprise, didn't you?' he said. 'Have you ever wondered if maybe you're in the wrong profession?'

She jerked her head around then to look at him, and he clapped a hand to his forehead, saying ruefully, 'I guess that's not the way I meant to put it. Only, for someone who's supposed to have given up sex, you've got an awful lot of passion locked up inside of you.'

'You . . . don't understand.'

'Damn right, I don't. Did you ever . . . commit that mortal sin?'

She shook her head. 'I don't want to talk about it; do you mind?'

He glanced at her and then looked back at what he was doing. He went out and wet the cloths once more, and soon the bleeding had stopped except for one tiny, deeper gash just above her right knee. He tore a couple of strips from the remainder of the shirt and bandaged that, then carefully pulled her skirt together, brushed a light kiss on her forehead and sat back.

'Thank you,' she said in a slightly strangled voice. That barely noticeable kiss had upset her equilibrium all over again. She had been right about Scott Carver. He was dangerous . . . infinitely dangerous . . . to her.

'Tell me about South America,' she said, picking a subject at random. 'About your Amazon expedition.'

He looked as though he knew exactly what she was doing, trying to distract them both from the memory of what had happened between them, but he shrugged and settled his shoulders against the bark and complied.

She was careful never to meet his eyes, and he didn't touch her again. When at last the howl of the wind abated and they dared to emerge, he let her climb down on her own, and they walked the rest of the way back to the mission, through devastated coconut groves and banana plantations that made her want to weep for the islanders and their livelihoods. They kept more than a foot of space between them all the way.

Chapter Five

The devastation was incredible. The whole island seemed to be flattened, trees lying in crazy heaps and houses minus roofs and walls, their supporting posts leaning at drunken angles, the simple household goods and furnishings scattered and broken.

The copra shed leaned at a peculiar angle and had lost some of its iron roof. Nearly all of the canoes, though they had been hauled ashore before the storm, were damaged or had simply disappeared. The yacht had snapped both her cables and been driven ashore and damaged, a hole torn in her hull and her radio badly smashed. The church and the hospital had remained standing, though missing pieces of the roof and guttering of the hospital were cause for concern, and some windows had been broken in spite of the precautions they had taken. The generator that kept the hospital supplied with electricity was intact, but the tank which stored the rainwater had been thrown from its stand and crushed, and the filtration and purification apparatus were beyond hope of repair.

Scott and Claire were welcomed with great relief, although Claire's appearance caused some anxiety at first. Sister Loretta hugged her, then held her away and said, grimacing, 'You do look a proper mess, don't you? What on earth have you been doing?'

'Climbing trees,' Scott answered for her. 'Just as well she knew about this particular tree, too. It had a hollow in it and probably saved our lives. She's got some nasty scratches under that bandage. You'd better make sure they're properly cleaned and dressed.'

'Yes, Mr. Carver, we will,' Sister Loretta assured him dulcetly as she ushered Claire inside, adding under her breath, 'They never do think that we've got any sense of our own, do they? Still, it's nice of him to be so concerned about you.'

Claire was thankful to get cleaned up, though with a minimum of water because of the accident to the tank, and submitted to having her wounds painted with iodine and a proper bandage put on the cut. But when Sister Loretta suggested that she should lie down, she refused. It was still light, and there was so much that needed to be done to alleviate the plight of the islanders. There was a queue of people with injuries received in the storm when they had stayed out too long trying to secure possessions or gather food before it was ruined, and she knew that every spare pair of hands was needed. Water had to be brought from several hundred yards away in a variety of containers and, for hospital use, boiled in Sister Martha's big pots and then cooled. It took time and strength, and was going to be a problem until the tank and filtration could be fixed.

Father Damien received the news of the breakdown of their only vehicle with a philosophical shrug. 'It wouldn't be much use at the moment anyway,' he said. 'The tracks will be blocked with fallen trees, and we don't have time to clear them. I'll send someone over on foot first thing in the morning to see if any help is needed on the other side, and meantime there's plenty to do here.'

'Looks like it,' Scott commented, surveying the nearby village, where the people were picking over the remains, trying to rescue what pitiful possessions they could, and a young mother rocked a bewildered, crying child in her arms beside their wrecked home. 'Where would you like us to start?'

He and the other men from the yacht spent the remainder of the day helping to find sheets of iron that could be used to repair the hospital roof, and nailing them in place in spite of the occasional gusty squalls of rain. Jess had organised the two other women from the boat into conducting a sort of creche in the hospital corridor, the only available space, for children whose parents and older brothers and sisters were trying to rebuild or repair their homes. Loretta, glancing out the door of the clinic where she and Claire were tending the injured, commented, 'It's amazing how a crisis brings out the best in people. I'd have sworn that that blond girl didn't have a thought in her head except how she looked and what kind of impression she could make on a man, and during the worst part of the cyclone she was hysterical with fright, but look at her now. I reckon she wouldn't make a bad little mother.'

Sheryl was sitting on a mat, her blond tresses tied up in a ponytail that made her look about twelve years old herself, while one small brown child occupied her lap and two others leaned against her shoulders, and she was showing them a magazine, explaining the pictures and making up stories.

Darlene didn't look so happy about her task. She chased a giggling toddler who was determined to escape from supervision, scooped him up and tucked him under her arm, her creamy skin red with exertion, and dumped him back in the group with a look of pure exasperation, saying loudly to Jess, 'Next time the little brat decides to run away, *you* can fetch him back!'

Still, she was helping, and Claire supposed there was probably more virtue in performing a task one didn't enjoy than doing something that was fun as well as useful.

Before nightfall the temporary repairs to the roof had been effected, and some of the men were boarding up windows with timber rescued from the various floating debris in the lagoon. Doug went back to the crippled yacht with Eddie Robson, who had insisted on discharging himself from the hospital, to see if they could fix the radio. The mission had a receiver, and when anyone had time to listen, they heard snatches of news about the hurricane's devastating path through the islands, but they could send no messages.

Later, when the patients had been fed, Sister Martha dished up a communal meal for the staff and the visitors in the kitchen, including the contents of some tins provided from the yacht's galley. The yacht, turned on its side, couldn't be used for sleeping, and room was made for the visitors in the living quarters of the hospital. The nuns doubled up to allow Darlene and Sheryl to share one of their rooms, and a mattress from the yacht was put in Claire's small room for Jess.

'I hope you don't mind this,' the dark girl said to Claire as they prepared for bed, trying to avoid bumping into each other in the limited space.

'No, of course not,' Claire replied as she pulled her light cotton nightdress on. She glanced at Jess, who wore a nightshirt that managed to look both casual and remarkably sexy at the same time. It gave a deliberate impression, Claire decided, that it was a garment borrowed from a lover, and yet it fitted Jess's lush but firm figure all too well.

Jess looked at her shrewdly. 'Of course you do, but you're too polite to say so. Well, it's only until the men can do something about the yacht, so I hope you won't get too fed up with me.'

'I'm sure I won't.'

Jess gave a low, attractive laugh. 'You really are polite! I was going to ask if you'd mind if I smoked, but you'd say no, and probably hate it, so I'll forgo that small pleasure tonight.'

'Please . . . not on my account,' Claire said. 'In fact . . . would you mind if I scrounged one, too?'

Jess's finely shaped eyebrows rose, but she pulled out a packet of filter-tipped cigarettes in a gold wrapper and offered one.

Claire very seldom smoked, but a friend had once persuaded her to try a cigarette when she was suffering from a tension headache, and it had worked. Now and then she had tried the cure again, and tonight she felt in dire need of its relaxing effect.

Jess lit both cigarettes with an elegant little gold lighter, then flicked it off and lay back on her mattress, blowing a plume of smoke toward the ceiling.

Claire drew on her own cigarette and said, 'Thank you. I shouldn't, I suppose, but I'll resist temptation another time.'

'I don't suppose you get much opportunity to be tempted. Isn't it deadly, living with a lot of nuns?'

'No. Actually, I'm used to it. I was brought up in a convent orphanage.'

'Really? Then you've always lived in a convent?' Jess regarded her curiously.

'No. I've lived in hostels and then a flat with some other girls for the last few years.'

'So what are you doing here, teaching the island kids and living with the sisters?'

'They needed a teacher. And I'm sort of on trial. I hope to be allowed to enter the convent when I get back to Sydney.'

'What on earth for?' Jess asked lazily.

'I wish people would stop asking me that,' Claire said, almost under her breath. She had never been questioned so often about her reasons before, except by Sister Josephine, who had at least had some sort of right.

'Sorry I asked,' Jess said.

Claire said quickly, 'No, it's all right. I didn't mean to sound rude. I suppose it's natural to be curious.'

'Are you some sort of novice or something?'

'No. That will come later.'

Jess smoked on in silence for a few moments and then said, 'I've never really known any nuns, but I wouldn't have picked you for one. You just don't strike me as the type. For one thing, you're far too pretty.'

'There isn't any type,' Claire said patiently. 'People don't enter the convent just because they can't get a man or because they've been crossed in love. Nuns are just like any other women, only they have a special . . .' she hesitated on the word 'vocation,' not sure if Jess would understand the particular meaning she ascribed to it, and substituted, '. . . a special . . . bent.'

Jess looked amused, turning her head to stare for a moment. 'Really? And are you . . . bent?'

Claire blinked, then flushed. 'No,' she said. 'That isn't what I meant.'

Jess sat up and leaned across the small space to put a hand on Claire's arm. 'Sorry!' she said. 'My cursed tongue. Look . . . I didn't mean it. It's like Scott said . . .'

'What did he say?' Claire asked so softly that she scarcely heard herself.

But Jess did. She leaned back again, drew on her cigarette deeply and exhaled with a sigh. 'It's a habit I've got into,' she said, 'baiting everybody, needling. I daresay it's very unattractive. Scott reckons it's a defence mechanism.' She grimaced. 'He's probably right, but what the heck. If it is, it's one I need.'

'Why do you need it?'

'To keep people at arm's length, sweetie, and stop me being hurt.'

Claire had hardly touched her cigarette, and the

ash was lengthening on the tip. She reached up to the narrow shelf over the bed and brought down one of the shells there, tipping the ash into it, then offering it to Jess.

Jess tapped her cigarette expertly on the edge of the shell and looked up. 'Thanks. You're easy to talk to, aren't you?'

'Am I?'

'Mm. You must have one of those faces that people instinctively trust.' Jess hitched herself up on the pillow and placed a hand behind her head, turning to subject Claire to her critical scrutiny. 'Although you're actually more than pretty . . . beautiful, even, in a cool, untouched sort of way. Except for the mouth. Felix said you had a "promising" mouth. I think I see what he means, too. It could drive a man wild, he reckoned.'

Claire looked fixedly at her cigarette and said distantly, 'I've no such ambition, I'm afraid. Anyway, I somehow don't think it would take much to drive Felix wild.'

Jess laughed. 'You'd be dead right, there. Very susceptible, is our Felix.'

She was looking upward, following the trail of smoke that curled towards the ceiling. The curve of her mouth looked cynical, and Claire was silent, remembering the lighthearted chase along the beach and then the passionate nature of the embrace Jess had exchanged with Felix. Fleetingly Claire wondered if Jess, too, was more susceptible than she liked to admit.

Then Jess brought her cigarette back to her lips and turned her head again to look at Claire, her expression quizzical. 'How did you get on with Scott, being stranded together like that? Did he make a pass?'

Claire took a quick drag on her cigarette. 'We talked.'

'Talked?' Jess repeated skeptically. 'What about?'

'Theology and life-styles.'

'Theology and . . .' Jess sat up and looked at her, eyes wide, the cigarette in her hand poised halfway to her mouth. Then she suddenly threw herself back on the pillow, howling with delighted laughter.

Claire watched in stunned silence, her cigarette burning slowly down between her fingers. A smile tugged at the corners of her mouth, and as Jess's laughter began to subside, she said mildly, 'Well, we did!'

'Oh, I believe you, sweetie! I believe you,' Jess told her, still laughing. She hitched herself sideways on the pillow, leaning on her elbow, and lifted the cigarette to her lips. 'All the same,' she said, 'I'll bet he made a pass at you.'

She was smiling, her eyes teasing wickedly.

Claire looked down at her cigarette, and Jess chuckled. 'Okay, don't tell me. It's none of my business.'

Carefully Claire said, 'You wouldn't mind?'

'Mind? No. Should I?'

'He said . . .'

'Scott said . . . ? Well . . . what?'

Claire shifted uncomfortably. 'That you'd been friends for years and . . . sometimes . . . more.'

'My,' Jess drawled. 'You certainly got talking, didn't you?'

Claire threw a glance of apology at her, and Jess said, 'Oh, it's okay. Yes, we're old friends, and now and then . . . Well . . . you know how things are.' After a wry glance at Claire's face, she said, 'Or maybe you don't. I don't know what kind of world you live in, but I guess it's nothing like mine.'

Hers and Scott's. Claire said, 'I guess not.'

'Sometimes I think it was a mistake,' Jess said slowly, 'being more than friends with Scott, even temporarily. We go way back, to before my divorce . . . before my marriage, actually. He had another lady then, and I was with the guy I married later. He and Scott knew each other. We used to go to the same parties, move in the same circle, and after my marriage broke up Scott was one of several people who were rather kind to me. He didn't come on to me, though, like some of the men. He seemed to know I didn't want that, and I don't think he did either. We were . . . friends, no hassle, no pressure, and it was nice that way. The other thing happened much later. . . . Once, when I was feeling down and alone, he came along, and one thing led to another, as they say. But it never really came to anything. I think he was doing me a favour. Later, I wished I hadn't . . . asked for it. All I'd wanted was an ego boost, and I felt rather beastly about making use of a good friend.'

She paused, then leaned over to press out her cigarette in the shell. 'Then there was a time when I felt I could return the favour,' she said. 'I practically insisted. And do you know what he said afterwards? Friends don't need to be repaid.'

'He was right,' Claire said softly.

'Of course he was right,' Jess admitted, throwing herself back on the pillow. 'That's why I hit him.'

Claire laughed. 'What did he do? Hit you back?'

'Scott? Never. He just walked right out on me. And didn't come back. Oh, we made it up later, but it's not quite the same. Now I use my "defence mechanisms" with him, too, and I didn't used to need them for Scott. I don't blame him for being fed up with me.'

'Is he?'

'He's told me so, sweetie. We've never pulled any punches between us. Mind, I think he's fed up with all of us this trip. He saw himself as the lone sea ranger, riding the waves and playing the intrepid explorer. But Darlene and Sheryl only want to see civilised ports where they can buy dresses and perfume, and even the men prefer to be able to get a decent haute-cuisine dinner now and then. The whole lot of them are bored to tears with tiny islands where there's nothing to do but swim and sunbathe and study the local customs. As darling Sheryl says, "But, Sco-o-ott! We can swim and sunbathe anywhere, and honestly, once you've seen one island you've seen them all! Crabs and palm trees and natives are so bo-o-o-ring!"'

Claire couldn't help smiling at Jess's wicked imitation of Sheryl's childish whine, though she tried to suppress it. Then she thought of Scott Carver saying, 'It only makes your mouth look deliciously kissable,' and leaned over hastily to add her cigarette butt to the other in the shell.

'You've got a wicked tongue,' she said, 'and I shouldn't listen.'

Jess laughed and got under the sheet, plumping up the pillow. 'I'd love to know what did happen between you and Scott today,' she said.

Claire switched off the light and said into the darkness, 'He thinks I'm a nun.'

For a moment there was a stunned silence; then Jess dissolved again in peals of laughter. 'Why?' she asked between giggles. 'Did you tell him that?'

'No,' Claire answered. 'I just didn't tell him any different.'

'Oh,' Jess gasped. 'You're priceless! Oh, this is marvellous!'

Claire didn't think it was marvellous. She thought it was fraught with danger and potential problems, but Jess's laughter was infectious, and it helped to put the whole episode into perspective. The man had made a pass, as Jess said, and nothing too drastic had resulted, after all. He would very soon forget all about it, as she must do. She must.

She went to sleep praying fervently that she would. And soon.

Sister Loretta was to visit the other villages and see if help was needed there, and in spite of his injured hand Father Damien decided to go too. He was concerned about the other members of his flock and, as he said, his legs still worked perfectly well, although the bandaged hand frustrated many of his efforts to help in cleaning up the debris and bringing some sort of order into the chaos left by the storm. Morris and Felix volunteered to accompany them and help to carry the medical supplies which Loretta might need, since the local villagers were fully occupied trying to cope with the aftermath in their own area.

The crops having been destroyed, the most urgent need, after fixing up some kind of shelter for everyone, was to salvage whatever they could that was still edible. Parties of islanders moved through the devastated banana groves hunting for bunches of fruit that could be picked up before they rotted and stored in the mission cool room, and heaps of coconuts, breadfruit and taro began to appear around the mission buildings. When the injured had all been dealt with and she had some time on her hands, Claire joined the 'scavengers' and soon became adept at spotting anything potentially useful among the ruined groves. Cooking utensils and mats and bowls could be found scattered among the trees, miles from the village, and these were filled with the fruit lying about among the uprooted trees and brought back to be reclaimed by their owners.

As she helped Sister Martha to sort the piles of fruit in the mission compound into baskets and fill the cool room, Claire was startled to see Scott bring in a square of pandanus matting filled with something and slung over his shoulder.

'Taro,' he explained. 'The plants were ruined, but the roots are edible, even if they weren't really ready yet for digging. Where do you want them?'

She showed him, leading the way into the cool room, where he helped her to place the vegetables in large nets hanging from the ceiling.

As they worked she tried to avoid his eyes, but couldn't help knowing that he was watching her a good deal of the time. Glad that she was wearing the head covering she usually donned for kitchen duty, she fingered it, nervously making sure that it was still in place.

'You've made it dirty now,' he said, and reached out a hand, perhaps to try to brush the dirt off.

Claire flinched, then saw his mouth thin with annoyance.

'I thought you were helping with the rebuilding,' she said.

'I was, but the manual labour is virtually over. Now it's on to thatching and weaving the roofs and walls. It's skilled work, and I'd only be in the way.'

He put a couple of the taro roots into a net, his hand brushing hers as she withdrew it. Claire turned hastily away to hide suddenly burning cheeks, fumbling among the pile of taro on the mat for more.

She was aware of a throbbing silence in the small, windowless room.

She stood up, hesitating before turning round, her hands full of taro. A hand closed on her upper arm and she jerked away, whirling to face Scott and snapping, 'Don't touch me!'

'I was only moving you out of the way so that I could get some more taro,' he said. Then he added deliberately, 'You didn't mind me touching you yesterday.'

'That's unfair!'

His eyes glittered with anger and something else. 'Maybe,' he agreed. 'It's also true.'

She stepped towards the net, and he reached out a casual hand, his fingers closing about the neck of the net so that she had to stop in front of him.

'Isn't it?' he insisted very softly, his eyes daring her to deny it.

'It was the storm . . . I wasn't acting normally.'

'I think you acted very normally. With your capacity for passion, do you call it normal to shut yourself away from life? Do you really think you can repress that side of your nature forever? Remember how you trembled when I touched you? How your mouth went soft and opened for me?'

She closed her eyes and whispered raggedly, 'Please . . . please stop this.'

His finger touched the skin of her cheek, then trailed across her lips and down the side of her neck until it met the small collar of her dress. Claire stood still, fighting a wave of sudden heat ignited by that light, fleeting touch.

He waited for the reluctant opening of her eyes. 'It wasn't just the storm, was it?' he said. 'You'd respond the same way right now if I kissed you.'

'No.'

'Yes!' He took a long, audible breath. 'I didn't intend to speak to you like this. But when I see you . . . when I remember . . . You know there's something between us. You've got to admit it!'

'All right, I admit it,' she said. 'But it doesn't mean anything. And it isn't going to go any further. It's like the cyclone, devastating while it lasts, but soon over. We were thrown together in peculiar circumstances, and you being the kind of man you are, and me being . . . being sexually frustrated,' she added bravely, 'I suppose what happened was inevitable.'

His brows rose slightly, a grim smile hovering about his mouth. 'So you admit that you're frustrated?'

'I suppose I must be. I'm still a woman, in spite

of . . . of the life I've chosen. Going on a diet doesn't make one less hungry, you know. But the results are worth the deprivation.'

He frowned. 'Are they?'

'Very much so,' she replied firmly. 'Now, please stand aside so that I can get on with this.'

For a moment she thought he would refuse, but then he removed his hand from the net and went straight out without stopping to help her finish.

She tipped the taro from her hands into the net and then clung to it for a few minutes, steadying herself. That display of coolness had been all on the surface. Inwardly she was shaking like a leaf, and her thoughts were in a turmoil.

The village elders had decided that all food was to be pooled and shared equally, and although the visitors were not included in the edict, Scott announced quietly that evening that the remaining stores from the *Bella Donna* would be added to the general total.

Some of the others looked askance at that, and it seemed that Darlene and her brother Doug might be going to object, but Scott stared back at them coolly with his brows raised, apparently daring them to say anything, and they changed their minds. Doug shrugged and turned away, and Darlene arranged her mouth into a sulky pout but said nothing.

'I'll clear some space in the storeroom for you,' Sister Martha said after Scott had brushed aside their thanks, and she bustled out to the annexe that adjoined the kitchen.

Jess, leaning against the long kitchen table with a cigarette held between her fingers, had been watching Scott with an enigmatic little smile playing about her mouth. When Scott and Doug had gone out to get the stores and bring them back while there was still some daylight, and Darlene and Sheryl, declaring themselves exhausted, had gone off to their small shared room, Jess stubbed out her cigarette in the sink and said to Claire, 'Scott's actually loving this, you know. He should have been a pioneer.'

'I'd have said a buccaneer,' Claire said involuntarily.

Jess eyed her interestedly. 'I would cast Felix in that role, except that he's developed a taste for soft living. Do you know, I suspect you've seen a side of Scott that I don't even know about?'

'Nonsense,' Claire said breathlessly. 'You've known him much longer than I have.' And much more intimately, her mind added.

'That doesn't always count for much,' Jess commented. 'Tell me, why are you wearing that thing round your head?'

Claire touched the white square and said, 'I always wear something to cover my hair when I'm helping in the clinic or the kitchen. It's more hygienic.'

'It also makes you look awfully like a nun,' Jess said dryly. 'I suspect I'm not the only one with defence mechanisms.'

Claire smiled, though her heart was hammering as if danger were imminent. 'It's only a defence against contaminating the food or the patients,' she said mildly, picking up a pile of plates to lift them onto a shelf. Jess and the other women had helped with the washing up, but there were still some plates and cups to be put away on shelves.

'Okay, have it your own way,' Jess said good-humouredly. 'Where shall I put these cups?'

Claire showed her, and Jess refrained from any more personal remarks.

The next day a light plane flew low over the island and circled it, apparently inspecting the damage, but it was impossible to tell if it was assessing it with a view to providing relief if it was needed, or only for the purpose of reporting the devastation for the news services. Father Damien and Felix returned later in the day, and everyone within earshot downed tools and came to hear what news they brought.

One person, Father Damien told them, had died when his house was hit by a tree, and another was missing, believed to have been swept out to sea by the fierce winds and drowned. Sister Loretta had treated many injuries and would stay on for a few more days to keep an eye on the more serious ones. Morris had stayed, too, and was doing what he could to help. The priest had administered comfort and aid where possible, conducted a funeral service for the dead man and led prayers for the one who was missing.

'It makes me feel very helpless, though,' he said tiredly at supper that evening. 'The people are remarkably cheerful, considering that most of them have lost their homes and crops. But I don't know what's going to happen to them when the present food supply runs out. At least two-thirds of the food crops have been ruined, I'd say.'

He looked up at Scott and said, 'How's the radio?'

Scott raised a questioning eyebrow in Doug's direction, only to receive a thumbs-down gesture.

'We did all we could, but the patient never recovered,' Eddie said. 'It's busted, and that's that. It won't run again without new parts.'

'I'm afraid the same goes for the Jeep,' Felix added bluntly. 'We found it on the way back and had a poke around the engine, but no luck. We can only bring it in with manpower, and I doubt if we'll get it going under its own steam again even if we do.'

'Don't bother,' Father Damien said. 'Manpower is needed for other things at the moment. I wish I knew how badly hit the other islands are. None of the bigger craft here is seaworthy at the moment, and I don't think anyone's got the time to worry about repairs.'

'The other islands are probably all in much the same state,' Scott said.

'I suppose so. I wonder how long it will be before some sort of relief from one of the larger centres can reach us. It would certainly be a big help if we could let them know somehow what's needed.'

'The medical supplies aren't going to last much longer,' Sister Amy told them. 'Dr. Adams was due to bring some more on her next visit, and we hadn't expected such a heavy usage in a short time. And, of course, the water supply is a real problem.'

'If we got the *Bella Donna* repaired,' Scott suggested, 'we could sail to one of the larger islands and let them know what you need . . . perhaps bring some supplies back.'

'That would be very generous of you,' Father Damien said. 'I'd expected that once your boat was ready to sail you'd be more than anxious to leave us for good.'

Scott smiled and shrugged. Jess leaned back in her chair and said drawlingly, 'He's enjoying himself, Father. I think Scott has always been a sort of frustrated Good Samaritan.'

Scott threw her a level look and said, 'You'd know all about that.'

Jess tipped her chin with a challenge in her eyes. 'Below the belt, Scott.'

'So pull your head in, lady,' he suggested pleasantly. 'You're liable to get it chopped off.'

Felix, Claire saw, was looking from Jess to Scott, a cynical smile hiding the hard gleam in his narrowed eyes.

'How soon do you think the yacht could be seaworthy?' Father Damien asked.

'What do you reckon?' Scott asked Eddie. 'A couple of days?'

'Should do it. We'll give it our best shot.'

Claire and Jess somehow ended up doing the dishes alone, the others having gone off in various directions. Jess was silent, and Claire said softly, 'Are you tired?'

'What sort of a dumb question is that?' the other woman snarled. Then, slamming a tea towel down on the bench, she added immediately, 'I take that back. You don't deserve my bad temper.'

Claire said easily, 'It's okay, really. You're right; it *was* a dumb question. We're all exhausted, and no wonder. You and the others have been surprisingly helpful.'

'Surprisingly?'

Claire shook her head and laughed, slightly embarrassed. 'My turn to apologise,' she said. 'Scott accused me of making judgements. It's a terribly bad habit. Arrogant, too.'

'He,' Jess said waspishly, 'has a few bad habits of his own. I shouldn't worry too much about what he says, if I were you.'

'I see he's not your favourite person at the moment. You nearly had a row at the table, didn't you?'

'Sometimes he just makes me so mad!'

'Yes. But you did start it, you know,' Claire pointed out.

'I suppose I did. My rotten tongue again. Even Felix told me the other day that it'll get me into trouble. And believe me, it isn't easy to get under his skin. He's a lazy devil.'

'What did you say to him?'

'Oh, something about being an overweight Lothario. He didn't like it.'

Claire smiled. 'I shouldn't think he would! Couldn't you have been a bit more tactful?'

'Tact is not my strong point,' Jess admitted, grinning rather sheepishly. 'Besides, at the time I was mad at him. He was coming on much too strong.'

'You didn't seem to mind that the first day . . . on the beach.'

'Oh, that!' Jess flicked the tea towel absentmindedly at a soap bubble sliding down a glass on the drainer. 'That was just a bit of silly horseplay. And in public. It couldn't have gone any further.'

Claire looked at her curiously, half-thinking that the other girl's tone was almost too casual. 'You mean . . . he couldn't get too close?'

'Literally!' Jess agreed dryly.

'That isn't quite what I meant.'

'I know what you meant,' Jess said abruptly, 'but cool it, will you? The last thing I need is to get involved with Felix. He practically has a different girl for every day of the week. You wouldn't wish that on me, would you?'

'I wasn't wishing anything on you,' Claire said. 'And if you don't want to talk about it, we won't. Shall we,' she suggested, tongue in cheek, 'discuss the weather instead?'

Jess gave her low, smoky laugh. 'The weather! Well, a cyclone is certainly some sort of weather to discuss.'

'It makes a change from "What a lovely day,"' Claire agreed, 'which is about all one can normally say about it, round here.'

Jess looked at her humorously. 'I like you,' she said unexpectedly. 'We're chalk and cheese, but I feel we're friends.'

Claire, letting the water out of the sink, turned to her and smiled. 'So do I. Isn't it odd?'

'Oh, I don't know,' Jess said, cocking her head to one side. 'It's . . . interesting.'

Scott came in just then, stopping in the doorway, his expression intrigued. 'What's so interesting?' he asked them, moving into the room.

'Claire and I have just decided that we're friends,' Jess told him.

'Is that a fact?' Scott said slowly. 'Is it allowed?' His glance flickered from Jess to Claire.

'Allowed?' Jess made a puzzled, half-laughing sound. 'What on earth do you mean?'

'I'm talking to Sister Claire,' Scott said. 'Do the rules let nuns have friends?'

Claire shot an appealing look at Jess, but she knew immediately that it was useless. Jess wasn't looking at her; she was regarding Scott with a teasing, triumphant smile. She was going to get back at him for having the last word at supper, and nothing would stop her. She let a small silence elapse for maximum effect, then said, 'But, Scott, darling! Claire isn't a nun! Whatever made you think that she was?'

Chapter Six

$\int$ cott said brusquely, 'Of course she's . . .'

Then he stopped abruptly, his eyes going from Claire's stricken face to Jess's knowing grin and then back again. His eyes narrowed sharply, and he said, much more slowly, 'Of course she's not.' And then, without moving that inimical gaze from Claire's face, he added grimly, 'And *she* did. Get out, Jess. I want to talk to . . . Claire.'

'I don't think she wants to talk to you, darling.'

He transferred that gimlet stare for a moment and snapped, 'Get lost!'

Jess moved instinctively, then stood her ground. 'Get lost yourself,' she said insolently. 'You needn't think you can order me around in that tone!'

Between his teeth he said, 'If you don't move of your own accord I'll . . .'

'Please, Jess,' Claire said swiftly. 'Go on.' Scott was obviously in a towering temper, and though he and Jess had sniped at each other before, they were old friends and she didn't want to become a bone of contention between them. Besides, she knew very well that Scott would have his explanation from her sooner or later.

'I won't leave you to the mercy of this oaf,' Jess assured her, a militant light in her eyes. 'He doesn't scare me!'

'It's all right,' Claire said. 'I'm not scared either. Please,' she repeated.

Jess looked at Scott, shrugged, and strolled with elaborate nonchalance to the door. 'Okay,' she said, 'but if you need help, yell. I'll be in the bedroom.'

'You and whose army?' Scott jeered at her.

'Oh, shut up!' she flashed at him before she closed the door with a bang.

'So you're not scared?' Scott said softly to Claire as soon as they were alone. 'Maybe you should be. I do not like being made a fool of.'

'I haven't made a fool of you,' she protested.

'You helped,' he said tersely. 'The rest of it I did all by myself, didn't I? Did you ever actually say you were a nun?'

'No. You jumped to conclusions.'

'Which you did nothing to rectify. Just the opposite, in fact. Are you going to tell me why?'

'It just seemed . . . easier.'

'That makes no sense,' he said crushingly.

'It's difficult . . . to explain.'

'Try.'

'Look, does it matter?' she asked, trying to sound casual.

'Yes,' he said. 'I think it does. It actually matters a hell of a lot to me. And don't expect me to apologise for my language,' he added as she glanced up at him. 'You can be thankful it's not worse. So tell me.'

'I . . .' She spread her hands despairingly. 'I can't.'

'You can.' He came nearer to her, making her step back so that she came up against the counter. 'And you can start by taking that thing off!' he added forcefully, twitching the cloth from her head.

Some fine nape hairs were caught in the knot, and she yelped with pain as they were pulled.

He looked at the cloth in his hand, a few pale strands clinging to it, and swore under his breath. He dropped the scarf and his hand came up behind her head to massage her nape, his fingers hard. 'I didn't intend to hurt you,' he said, 'although I admit it's a temptation.'

His eyes were still points of angry fire, and she shivered under his touch.

'You always do that,' he said softly. 'Every time I touch you. Do you know what a turn-on it is?'

She tried to shake her head, mesmerised by his eyes and his fingers massaging her skin under her hair.

'Why did you pretend?' he asked her, and as she tried to avoid his eyes, his hand shifted slightly, bringing her head up so that she had to look at him.

'I . . . was afraid. . . .'

A frown appeared between the glittering blue eyes. 'Why? You think I'm some sort of sex maniac?'

She managed a slight negative sign, her eyelashes lowering to her cheeks.

'I don't use force on women,' he murmured. 'I

wouldn't have made you do anything you didn't want to.'

She shut her eyes, aware that what had frightened her most had been her own wants, her own totally unexpected responses.

His hand propelled her closer, and he moved forward so that their bodies touched. She felt his breath on her forehead, and then his lips lightly touched each eyelid, before moving to her mouth as his other hand found the curve of her waist, holding her against him.

She tried to say no, but the sound was lost in his mouth, in a kiss that was tender and compelling at the same time, willing her surrender to him.

She stood quiescently in his arms, allowing herself to be kissed, savouring the feel of his chest pressing on her breasts, his hand stroking her back, and most of all the taste of his mouth on hers. But she didn't kiss him back, didn't put her arms about him or respond at all. She felt powerless in every way, unable to stop him from doing what he wanted, although his hold was not in the least coercive and she might have broken away with ease. Yet in one corner of her mind she was dully aware that there was no future in this, that allowing him to make love to her completely could only destroy her peace, and that she must not let it go any further.

He drew back, and with his hands on her waist said quietly, 'I feel as though I'm kissing a rag doll. It wasn't like this yesterday.'

'I'm sorry to disappoint you,' she said, her voice husky and uneven. 'It isn't ever going to be like yesterday.'

'Would you like to bet on that?'

His arms drew her to him again, and she put her hands against him, holding him off. 'Please!' she said. 'I'm really not interested in being one of your . . . your passing parade of women!'

His hands tightened, and he said, 'You know nothing about me . . . or my women.'

'I know enough,' she said, her body stiffening in resistance. 'You said yourself that if it had been any other girl with you, you'd have been making love to her.'

'That isn't what I said.'

'It's near enough. I don't want to join in your games. It . . . it just isn't my scene.'

'Yesterday wasn't a game. Not for me, and not for you, either. Was it?'

He held her shoulders as though he would have shaken her, and she said, 'Yesterday was a *mistake!*'

'I don't think so.'

'I don't care what you think,' she said stubbornly. 'I'm not going to let you ruin my life!'

'I don't intend to,' he said impatiently.

'But you would!' She held his eyes resolutely, trying to get through the angry, baffled desire and speak to his mind. 'It might not be true yet that I'm a nun, but I'm going to be. I've made the decision, and I'm not going to change my mind.'

'What do you mean, you've made the decision?' he demanded. 'When?'

'Before I ever came here. I would have entered last year, but Mother Josephine—the mother superior—thought that . . .'

'That what?'

'Never mind. They needed a teacher here urgently, so I came for a year. When I leave here it will be to enter the convent.'

'Over my dead body!' he said fiercely.

Suddenly angry herself, she cried, 'What's it to you? Don't tell me you care about me! You only care about your own selfish pleasure. You got yourself a new thrill yesterday, that's all. Something different to add to your list of . . . adventures. I suppose it was pretty naïve of me to imagine that thinking I was a nun would deter you. To someone like you it probably only added a touch of spice.'

His eyes went cold, his face taut. 'I wouldn't have touched you,' he said brutally, 'if you hadn't practically begged me to.'

She gasped. 'I *didn't!*'

'Yes you did, and you know it. Not in so many words, but with your eyes and your body you were screaming for me, you poor frustrated little *nun*. And then in the end you were too scared to follow through.'

She turned her head away, humiliated beyond bearing, and tried to free herself from his grip. He released her shoulders, only to cup her head in his hands, holding her firmly and brushing his thumbs over her hot cheeks. 'You weren't meant to be celibate, Claire,' he told her. 'You were made for loving.'

When she was very young she had been taught that everyone was made to love and serve God. 'There are different ways of loving,' she said, trying to evade his touch, but her hands on his wrists had no effect. 'What you're talking about isn't love.'

'It can be,' he said. 'One way of loving.'

'Not for me. Let me go.'

'You're trembling again.' Little lights were flickering in the blue depths of his eyes, like points of flame. His voice was low and soft, incredibly seductive.

'Please,' she said, her eyes half-closing in distress. 'Let me go.'

'And if I do,' he said, 'you'll go away from me.'

'Yes.' She swallowed. 'I must.'

His hands moved to her shoulders. 'Fleeing temptation, Claire?'

'If you want me to admit that you're a temptation,' she said wearily, 'then yes. You are, and I am.' She tried again to escape his hold, and his fingers tightened almost painfully.

Meeting his eyes with an effort, she said, 'You told me you didn't use force on women.'

His mouth twisted. 'For you, I could make an exception.'

Their eyes locked for long, aching seconds. Then he suddenly stepped back and she was free.

'Are you really going into a convent?' he asked her.

'Yes.'

'Dream of me sometimes,' he said, 'when you're sleeping in your narrow little virginal bed. There can't be any sin in dreams, can there?'

She didn't answer, but clenched her teeth on a sudden wave of warmth that suffused her body at the provocative words, the caressing tone of his voice.

With his hand on the knob of the outer door he turned to look at her again, his eyes sweeping over her body in a look as intimate as a touch. 'I won't forget you, my little nun,' he said. 'I might even have dreams of my own.'

Jess looked at her curiously when she came into the bedroom and flung herself down on the bed.

'You look as though you've had a rough time,' she commented. 'What did he do to you?'

'Nothing.' Claire closed her eyes, willing the tears not to gather under the lids.

'Want me to go away so you can cry it out?' Jess asked.

Claire shook her head.

After a while Jess said, 'I'm actually dying of curiosity, of course. I don't think I've ever seen Scott quite so mad before. What's it all about?'

'He just doesn't like to look foolish. He felt a bit silly when you told him. . . .'

'Look,' Jess said, 'I'm sorry if I dropped you in it. I wanted to score a point off him, but he could always take a joke. I never thought he'd take it out on you.'

'It wasn't your fault. He'd have found out sometime, I suppose.'

'What's the matter with him, anyway? There *is* something between you two, isn't there? What happened out there in the storm?'

'Nothing happened. Nothing . . . world-shattering. He's just a bit annoyed that he made a silly mistake about me and I didn't put him right.'

'That wouldn't put him into a rage like I saw tonight, dear girl, but if you don't want to tell me, you won't. I'll even be noble and promise not to try to worm it out of Scott. How's that for friendship?'

Claire had to smile. 'Thanks,' she said, opening her eyes, 'but I don't suppose you'd have a hope if Scott didn't want to tell you.'

Jess grimaced. 'You're dead right there. I wouldn't.'

She fished a pack of cigarettes from under her pillow and offered it. 'Have one?'

Claire hesitated, then helped herself. 'You're leading me into bad habits,' she murmured as Jess lit it for her.

Jess put the flame to her own cigarette before she answered, 'Two cigarettes in two days won't make you an addict.' She lay back, her hands playing with the cigarette packet, turning it in her long, elegant fingers. 'You're going to get into a good habit soon enough, aren't you?' She laughed and added, 'Sorry, that was a terrible pun. You're not offended, are you?'

'Of course not.'

'It must be nice,' Jess mused, 'to have your life mapped out, to know exactly what you're going to do for the rest of your days.'

'Yes,' Claire said. 'It's a very comforting thought.'

'Lucky you.' Jess drew on her cigarette and blew a series of perfect smoke rings towards the ceiling. Claire watched, then applauded softly. 'My one talent,' Jess told her. 'The only thing I've ever learned to do properly.'

'I don't believe that.'

'It's true. I mess up everything else. You've no idea how I envy you, Claire. You've got it all together, haven't you?'

Claire didn't answer. Jess couldn't know that at the moment she felt anything but 'together.' Her brain, her body, were in turmoil, one going over and over the same arguments, the other still remembering the warm masculine taste of Scott's mouth, the feel of his hard body against hers.

But Jess didn't wait for a reply. 'I've spent my life,' she said, 'falling for the wrong guys and making the wrong decisions. You'd think I'd have learned after the first time, wouldn't you? But not me. I just go right on doing stupid things.'

With sudden insight Claire said, 'Like falling in love with Felix?'

Jess took her cigarette from her lips and regarded the glowing tip with concentration. Finally she said softly, 'It's that obvious, huh?'

'No. It only just occurred to me. I know he's . . . interested in you, though.'

'Oh, sure. He's interested in anything in skirts, on a strictly short-term basis. Felix is not exactly selective. And he's definitely not the faithful type.'

'And you are?'

'I've had enough of playing around. I thought that was the answer . . . Oh, heck! You want to know the whole sordid story?'

'Only if you want to tell me.'

Jess looked at her, her green eyes brilliant and concentrated. 'I think I do,' she said slowly. 'Maybe it will help me to sort myself out.'

She reached for the shell ashtray, stubbed out her cigarette and sat cross-legged on the mattress as she lit another. 'Well,' she said. 'Ten years ago . . . I was eighteen . . . how long ago that seems! I fell for a married man. Oh, I didn't know that, at first. It's the old story. It never occurred to me that he wasn't free, and when I asked, he said he was divorced, or nearly. He had two children, and he was seeing them—that was why he wasn't always free to be with me. So I let it ride while I thought about marrying a divorced man with children—because he said he wanted to marry me. And then he told me she—the wife he was supposed to have been separated from for ages before he'd met me, who wanted a divorce as much as he did, so he'd said—was pregnant. Do you know, I was so stupid that I thought at first it couldn't be his! What an idiot. And of course no way was he going to break up his marriage then! The perfect alibi. He seemed to think I should admire his noble attitude. But what really made me sick was the fact that he didn't seem to realise that it changed things. You should have heard him. . . . How could I be so selfish, when everyone could be perfectly happy if we just carried on as we were, a cosy threesome . . . only of course his wife didn't know about me.'

'And you wouldn't agree to that,' Claire said.

'No, I wouldn't. I broke my heart over that . . . that pig. Even though by then I knew he wasn't worth it. And then Denny came along and picked up the pieces. I'd thought Tom was pretty special, handsome, witty, charming. Denny was all that and more. He was kind, too, and rich. Sounds mercenary, but I didn't really think of it that way. He wasn't ostentatious about his money, but it smoothed the way, and I felt I'd had it rough long enough. My family had never been well off, and my job was a dead-end clerk's position with a small wage. When Denny asked me to live with him, I hardly thought twice. My mother disapproved, and

Dad hasn't spoken to me since, but I figured I had nothing to lose. . . .

'So I lived with him. I thought I was happy, and when I found out I was pregnant, and told him I didn't want an abortion, he offered to marry me. I knew he didn't really want to, but he was basically a decent bloke. And I was thrilled. Maybe deep down every woman does want a home and family of her own. Anyway, I guess I did.'

'What went wrong, then?' Claire asked as Jess paused to puff rather quickly on her cigarette.

'I lost the baby. I can't even do that right, you see,' Jess said bitterly. 'Poor Denny, he'd psyched himself up to marry me and start a family, and almost as soon as we'd tied the knot . . . there wasn't going to be any family, after all.' She paused, and added huskily, 'Not ever. There were complications, and by the time they'd finished fixing me up, they told me I'd never be able to have another child.'

'Oh, Jess! How awful for you.'

'Yes, it was rather. I hadn't really thought of myself as the maternal type. Even when I found out I was having Denny's baby, I think it was more the prospect of being able to hold Denny than the thought of the baby itself that made me want it. But when it died . . . I hadn't known that anyone could feel grief like that for such a . . . a *little* life.'

'I'm so sorry, Jess.'

Jess smiled at her. 'Oh, I got over it in time. But it was too late for Denny and me. Our relationship had been a fun thing from the beginning, and I was no fun anymore. For months I was depressed, weepy, hopelessly dreary for anyone to live with

. . . especially someone like Denny. And I didn't even . . . I'd lost all interest in sex.' Her mouth turned down bitterly. 'So, naturally, Denny found someone else. I don't really blame him, but at the time it seemed to be the last straw. There must have been something about domesticity that he'd grown to like, because he desperately wanted to marry his new girlfriend. I gave him the divorce he asked for, in return for a handsome amount of alimony which I've been living on ever since. If I have nothing else, at least I'll have money, I thought. And it helps . . . when you don't have anything else. I began to have fun again, but I was careful not to involve myself too deeply.'

'Afraid of being hurt again?' Claire suggested.

'Yes, I suppose so. That's when Scott . . . Well, you know about that. Sometimes I wish I had fallen in love with him.'

'Would he have been any better?' Claire asked skeptically. 'He isn't a one-woman man either, surely?'

'He's played the field a bit. But I have the feeling that once he made a real commitment to a woman, he'd stick to it, no matter what. Though who am I to judge?' Jess added wryly. 'I've just confessed to being an awfully bad picker. Anyway, it's wishful thinking. Scott's never been in love with me.'

'Has he been in love with anyone?'

'I don't know.' Jess frowned. 'He had one long-term affair, I know, but the lady walked out on him. He was pretty disillusioned at the time. That's when I did my comforting bit.'

Claire was longing to know more, but she consciously directed her mind back to Jess's problems.

'And now you've picked Felix,' she said. 'I don't know him well, but . . .'

Her voice trailed off doubtfully, and Jess said, 'Yes, *but* . . . Felix is the take-what-you-want-and-walk-away-whistling sort of man. There must be something wrong with me, something that draws me to the wrong kind of guys. The trouble is, he's much too experienced not to know that I'm attracted to him, no matter how much I pretend otherwise. And he's not above taking advantage of it. I don't know how much pressure my willpower can stand.'

'Perhaps you need a chaperone.'

'Oh, Sheryl is quite willing to fill that role. When I'm not hating that girl, I feel quite sorry for her. She's out of her depth with Felix, and why he had to drag her along . . . ! She bores him to tears and the rotten skunk lets her know it. Men really are the end. Sometimes I think we'd all be better off without them. You've got the right idea.'

Claire smiled. 'Maybe. But convent life wouldn't suit everyone. I . . . hope you're not looking for good advice from me, because I honestly don't know what to say.'

'No, I have to work it out myself. It's helped talking about it, though.' Jess killed her cigarette with a decisive gesture. 'Thanks, Claire.'

'You're welcome.'

Claire lay in the darkness for a long time after they had put the light out, wondering if it would have helped her to confide in Jess. For the first time since she had made the decision to enter the convent, she was having serious doubts about her vocation. *You weren't made for celibacy*, Scott had told her. Was he right? Did that devastating capacity for passion which he had discovered mean that she was unsuited to the life she had chosen? She turned to lie on her stomach, hiding her hot face in the pillow. Was she capable of a lifetime of repressing the raging need that had been aroused in her?

But surely in time it would ease, become no more than a faint, painful memory. She turned onto her back again, restlessly, and her eyes sought and found the small crucifix that was fixed above the doorway, gleaming in the moonlight that fell on it. She began a tormented prayer, and gradually her blood cooled and a sort of peace descended on her. She felt that she was no longer alone with her terrible doubt and fear, and finally fell asleep, convinced that with prayer and patience she would be certain of finding the right answer.

The men worked on the yacht all Friday and Saturday, helped by some of the island boatbuilders, who recommended the gum of the breadfruit tree as a waterproof adhesive on the joins and lent their expertise. By Saturday evening they had finished patching the hole in the hull, but it was felt that the repair should be given twenty-four hours to dry and set before the *Bella Donna* was launched. Jess told Claire that Scott and Eddie suspected that the advice was given at least partly because of the islanders' strict notions of keeping the Sabbath. In spite of the urgency of the need, they might have felt uneasy about helping to launch the boat on Sunday. 'We'll get her in the water first thing Monday morning,' Scott said to Father Damien. 'There'll be seven fewer mouths to feed, anyway, and if you give me a list of what's most urgently needed, I'll make sure that it's flown in. There must be planes ferrying emergency supplies.'

'It's very good of you,' Father Damien told him.

'Rubbish. It's the very least we could do. Thank you for your hospitality, and the shelter from the storm. Thanks . . .'—his glance swept round the table, skimming over Claire with the rest—'to all of you.'

He was going away, she thought with numbing clarity. She would never see him again.

This is stupid, she told herself, unable to believe that the prospect could affect her so deeply. She had only known the man a few days, had not even liked him for most of them. She couldn't possibly be in love with him.

Even if she changed her entire life for his sake, gave up her dream of being a nun and offered herself to him, he would take her and leave her, if not here, then somewhere else. Wherever they happened to be when he got tired of her.

She would never throw away her whole life's training, her deepest beliefs and principles, for any man, she told herself, even while her heart demanded treacherously, *Not even for this man?*

No, not even for this man. Firmly she pushed temptation aside.

On Sunday Scott and Jess came to church, sitting at the rear as though they preferred not to be noticed, but the courteous islanders made room for them and welcomed them with shy smiles. Sister Loretta, starting early that morning with a large group of islanders, had made the trek back to the mission in time for Mass. She looked tired, but insisted on taking a shift in the hospital, allowing Sister Amy to have a rest. Claire, carefully avoiding any chance of meeting Scott, stayed around the hospital too, trying to relieve the two nuns of some of the extra work. The twins that had been born on the day of the storm were small and sickly; their mother, too, was not strong, and her condition caused some concern. Sister Amy wanted all of them watched constantly. Claire was able to do that for her, sitting by the mother and her babies, ready to call for one of the nurses at any sign of unusual symptoms in the two tiny forms, and keeping a covert eye on the mother as well.

Trying to concentrate on that vital task, she was able to forget about her personal turmoil for minutes at a time. She stayed through evening prayers, and then Sister Martha relieved her, insisting that she had done enough and should rest.

In bed, she tried again to pray, but all she could think of was that Scott was lying on his makeshift bed in the clinic anteroom, and that the next day he would be gone from her life forever.

The night was hot and still, and Jess stirred restlessly in her sleep, flinging off the sheet that covered her and throwing one arm above her head.

The sound of the distant breakers hurling themselves against the reef was the only noise Claire could hear, except her own uneven breathing. Through the open window came the heavy, sweet odour of rotting vegetation, coconuts and soft fruits, mingling with the scents of gardenia and frangipani.

At midnight she looked at her watch and could bear it no longer. She got out of bed, quietly snatched up a sarong of printed cotton and wrapped it about her waist over her thigh-length nightgown, then stealthily opened the door, sliding through and closing it very quietly behind her.

The lights in the hospital were out; only a pale yellow glow from Sister Amy's desk lamp showed through the window as Claire left the building.

The moon was washing everything in soft light, the slight grassy slope in front of the mission buildings stretching to the white shore and the quiet edge of the lagoon, cobbling its rippled surface with silver.

The church was in darkness, although she could see the faint red glimmer of the sanctuary lamp, signifying the presence of the blessed communion host in the tabernacle on the altar. She went in and knelt near the doorway, asking for guidance and help. But found no sense of the presence of God, and her prayers seemed to fall into a vacuum. The building was full of shadows, in spite of the oil flame flickering behind its red glass, and she shivered and returned to the empty night outside.

The stars were a canopy of jewel points flung over the island and out to sea, the moon hanging like a great fluorescent disk above her. She remembered that Scott had said that sometimes in the night, between the ocean and the stars, he had felt close to believing in God.

Where is God?

God is everywhere.

The question and answer came to her mind from the nearly forgotten lessons of her childhood. Religion classes with Sister Josephine, Sister Alberta, Sister Margaret Mary . . . For a moment she was sick with longing for the safe, secure rituals of childhood and the loving, disciplined care that the sisters at the convent had given her.

She walked across the moonlit grass to the shore, staring at the *Bella Donna,* still tipped on her side, the new patch uppermost on her hull. There were no lights and one of the vessel's masts stood starkly at an angle against the moon. Blindly Claire began to walk towards the sea, its salty tang and the gentle whisper of the waves drawing her.

The storm had littered the foreshore with seaweed and debris, and she avoided the dark heaps, the sarong brushing against her ankles, her feet soundless on the gritty sand, wandering aimlessly.

She walked for a long time, the sea shushing at her feet, the warm air brushing her bare shoulders. A clump of trees barred her way, and she skirted them, not going up on the grass, but lifting the sarong to her thighs and splashing through the water to the other side and the hidden little bay.

With a sudden shock of familiarity she looked about and realised that this was where Scott had caught her after her swim. There seemed to be little damage here. In daylight the hibiscus might be tattered, the leaves stripped from some of the trees, but in the kindness of the dark she could see no change.

She waded out onto the sand and turned to face the sea. The mingled scents there were almost overpowering, the flowers that had survived the storm giving off perfumes that mingled with the strong pungency of coconut and sun-warmed vegetation, and the sharp salty smell of seaweed.

The warm, moist tropical air dewed her upper lip with fine perspiration, but the water drying on her skin cooled her legs, and she wished that she had thought to bring her bikini.

But of course no one was about, nor would anyone ever know if she swam naked. The prospect was infinitely enticing; the shortage of water at the mission meant that everyone could have only the most cursory of baths, and she had been too busy that day to bathe in the sea. She tugged at the knot on the sarong and pulled it off, then let it fall to the sand, catching the air and ballooning a little before it spread itself in a dark patch at her feet.

She stripped off the nightgown and without hesitation walked into the water, pausing at the edge to let it lap about her ankles, then wading boldly in and, when it reached her thighs, launching herself into its silken embrace.

She dived and swam underwater, then surfaced and floated gently for a long time, not exerting herself but wallowing in the sensuous delight of the water buoying her up and caressing her bare skin. Occasionally she would turn and swim a few strokes parallel to the shore, but most of the time she lay on her back, now and then moving her arms lazily, allowing the water to support her while her eyes were fixed on the stars scattered overhead.

Gradually her unhappy tension eased and a sense of fatalism took its place, a fatalism not unmixed with pain. She no longer felt abandoned and alone, adrift on a stormy sea. Somewhere there was a safe harbour, and someday she would find it.

She came out of the water as the man emerged from the trees, and her heart lurched with fright, then settled into a steady, suffocating beat. She knew it was Scott even before the moonlight caught his fair hair and burnished his shoulders. There was a sense of inevitability about his being there at that moment. He wore dark pants and no shirt, his feet were bare, and he was coming to meet her.

She stood where she was, just above the water-line, her hands by her sides. She didn't even attempt to cover herself.

He stopped by the shadowy shape of the sarong and stooped to pick it up. Then he stood waiting for her, the piece of cloth in his hands. She walked slowly up the sand, knowing he was watching every step, her head held high, her tread firm. As she drew closer she could see the taut expression on his face and the hard line of his mouth. She stopped before him, not reaching for the sarong but letting him see her, letting his eyes take in her body in its nakedness.

He moved and brought the sarong up, wrapping it about her with an almost reverent touch. He brought the edges together at the front and stopped with his knuckles hard against her skin, pressing on the soft flesh. 'I watched you,' he said. 'You're very beautiful. I waited and willed you to come, and told myself that if you did, it was a sign.'

'You saw me go into the water?'

'Yes. Don't ask me to say I'm sorry I watched. I can't be sorry.'

Claire shook her head, an almost infinitesimal movement, but it brought a shower of water onto her shoulders, running down her skin, until he felt the drops against his hands. He looked down and carefully folded one end of the sarong over the other, and tucked it in. His fingers drifted over her back and onto her shoulders. 'There's a phosphorescence on the water,' he said. 'You were outlined in molten gold. Your arms, your body . . . your breasts.'

'Scott . . .' she breathed. His hands caressed her as he described it, and she felt bathed in fire, his touch a flame. Trying to hold on to her sanity, she said, 'I must go back.'

'There's no going back,' he said, and his hands came up to her face, cupping it between them, making her look at him, his mouth determined, his eyes lit with desire. 'You came to me. You had to come, just as I had to wait for you. There are no more choices to make, Claire.'

Her body was crying out silently with need, her mind confused. 'No!' she whispered as his mouth came down to hers, his eyes fixed on her parted lips.

As if the denial had angered him, he claimed her lips without mercy, his mouth insisting on a total surrender, one hand sliding down her back to bring her close to him. She lay against him helplessly, her hands clinging to his shoulders, her head fallen back against his arm. His other hand came up and tugged at the sarong until it slid to her waist, and with a deep groan of satisfaction he took her breast in his palm.

She shivered in his arms and twisted her head away from his kiss, a startled, sighing gasp forcing itself from her throat. Tiny pearl drops of water fell from her hair and slid along the skin of her neck and trickled farther down. He shifted both hands to her waist, holding her away for a moment, his eyes on her averted face as she tried in anguish to beat back a rising tide of desire. He watched the passage of the errant droplets and bent his head to trail his lips after them until his mouth reached her breasts, and he pulled her closer, ignoring her sudden cry of strangely mingled distress and pleasure.

His hands at her waist locked her to him, and his mouth returned to hers, urgent, tender and compelling, until she gave in with a small, despairing sound in her throat and opened her lips, giving him access to the softness inside.

As the sarong slipped lower his hands roamed over her back and hips. She felt his thumb fleetingly press into the hollow of her navel as his fingers spread across her stomach. Ripples of pleasure chased each other over her skin, and she sighed again into his ravaging mouth.

His hand slid over her waist and rib cage to take her breast again, and with a last effort at resistance she closed her fingers about his wrist, trying to dislodge it. But as his thumb and fingers teased at the soft flesh, her hand instead covered his and pressed it urgently against her, and her body of its own volition curved itself to him, yearning unmistakably for his possession.

Recognising her final surrender, he loosened the sarong from her hips, and even while he kept on kissing and touching her, spread it under them as he bore her down to the ground. She opened her eyes and saw the stars, high and bright and distant behind him, and his face, intent and almost gaunt with naked passion.

She stiffened, a frisson of fear and sudden awareness of what was about to happen cooling her hot skin. But then he took her fully in his arms, the rough cloth of his trousers against her thighs contrasting with the surprising smoothness of his back under her palms. He touched her lips softly with his, and then trailed his mouth to the shallow groove below her ear. 'Don't be scared,' he whispered to her. 'I swear I won't hurt you.'

And he began to caress her body with the gentlest of fingertips, and to kiss it, touching her more and more intimately until she was totally engulfed in pleasure, her head moving from side to side as she moaned and whimpered and dug her outflung hands into the sand at either side, and then brought them back to clutch at him and press his head to her damp skin. When he discarded the remainder of his clothing and joined her in her nakedness she welcomed him into her arms and scarcely noticed the shaft of distant pain that accompanied the ultimate consummation, when at last he brought her dizzily flying straight into the stars.

Chapter Seven

They lay quietly, still partially entwined in the aftermath of passion, his hand at her waist and his mouth against her temple.

'I knew it,' he said with soft exultation. 'I knew it would be different with you.'

He shifted to her side, leaning on one elbow, and bent over to kiss her closed eyelids and feather another kiss over her mouth. 'Are you all right, darling?' he whispered when she made no response.

She turned her head away from him and felt him go very still. 'Claire?'

Tears squeezed from beneath her tightly shut lids, and as he put a hand to her face he felt them trickling onto his fingers. 'Claire?' he said again, urgently. 'I didn't hurt you, did I?'

She managed a choked whisper. 'No.'

She wished, almost, that he had. She wished that she had summoned the strength to fight him so that he could have taken her only by force. Then she would have been spared the dreadful blackness of the guilt that now overwhelmed her.

He said, 'Don't cry. Don't spoil it. It was beautiful . . . wasn't it?'

Beautiful . . . yes. No other word could have described her feelings in his arms a few moments earlier. It had been both beautiful and terrible. Never had she imagined herself capable of such depth of feeling, such abandonment to pleasure, such joy in a man's body . . . in her own.

He licked at the salt tears on her cheek and said, 'Some people feel sad afterwards. The French call it *tristesse.*'

'I know what the French call it,' she said bitterly.

She turned away again and flung an arm over her eyes.

He stopped touching her, and soon she sensed that he had gone from her side. She didn't move, but in a few moments he gently pulled away her arm and washed the tearstains with a cool, dampened handkerchief. He touched her thighs and said, 'You've still got those scratches,' and washed her there, too.

She shivered and moved her head restlessly. Her hair was coated with sand, and as he sat back, balling the handkerchief in his hand, she got up suddenly and went down to the water like someone in a trance.

The lagoon received her like a balm. She held her breath and went under, emerging yards from the shore, and began to swim straight out to the narrow white line that marked the reef.

She didn't realise that he had followed her until she saw him pacing her a few feet away. She dived again and stayed down until her lungs ached with an irresistible need for air, then emerged gasping.

In a moment he was beside her, grabbing at her, a handful of hair in each fist. 'What are you trying to do?' he demanded. 'Drown yourself?'

'I wish I could!' she said starkly. 'Let me go!'

He released her, and she turned and made for shore, staggering up the sand but refusing his hand, which was outstretched to help her. She picked up the sarong and wrapped it about her wet body, then searched for and found her discarded nightdress, folding it with unthinking precision.

Scott had pulled on his trousers and was buckling his belt as she began to walk away.

'Where are you going?' he demanded.

Tight-lipped, she kept walking until his hand on her arm stopped her.

His voice harsh, he said, 'I didn't rape you.'

'No,' she agreed stonily.

He frowned down at her, his face filled with frustration. 'I'll walk you back,' he told her, as though he expected an argument and wasn't going to tolerate it.

But Claire only shrugged indifferently and shook herself free of his hold before she walked on.

Once she tripped over a piece of driftwood hidden in the sand, and his hands shot out to catch her against him. His breath was warm on her forehead, and her hands closed into fists against his bare chest. 'Darling,' he said softly, his voice almost a moan, his fingers tightening on her arms.

But she fought him almost frenziedly. *'Don't touch me!'*

She backed away from him, and he raised his hands with an exaggerated gesture. 'Okay, okay. But for heaven's sake, Claire . . . Was it *so* wrong?'

'Yes!'

The fierceness of the single word stopped him in his tracks. He spread his hands and said, 'I can't believe that.'

Her voice was harsh and unsteady. 'You don't believe anything, do you? Except in getting what you want, when you want it. I *said* no! Why couldn't you have listened to me?'

'Because your body was saying *yes,* loud and clear! I knew, and *you* knew, what you really wanted! The same thing that I did!'

She turned and began to run across the littered sand, dodging the piled seaweed and debris, fleeing from him, from the dark demons he represented. The mission buildings loomed ahead, and she raced over the sparse sandy grass into their shadow.

He was there, too, beside her as she reached the door, his hand on her arm, spinning her round to face him.

Her breathing was loud and uneven, and he held her until it steadied. 'Look,' he murmured, keeping his voice down. 'We can't talk here. Come to the church.'

In the circumstances, that seemed sacrilegious to her. She shook her head vehemently, trying to fight free of his hands.

'Claire!' he said more loudly.

She made herself be still then, because she didn't

want them to be heard. She stayed sullenly in his hard hands, with her face averted from him while he tried to read it in the shadow of the doorway.

At last he said, 'You're all wrought up. I'm sorry if it's so traumatic for you. . . . I'm sorry.' He paused, then added, 'Look, we'll be leaving early in the morning, but I'll come back. I'll be back just as soon as I can. . . . I promise. We'll talk then. Okay?'

She didn't answer, would give him no sign.

He let out a long, exasperated breath and caught her head in his hands, forcing her mouth to meet his.

His kiss was long and hard and angry, and it woke no response in her. When it was over he sighed again and pushed her inside, saying, 'Remember, I'll be back.'

The damp sarong was lying on the floor in the morning, and Jess eyed it curiously as they dressed before dawn in readiness for the early launching of the *Bella Donna*.

'Been swimming already?' she queried.

'I couldn't sleep,' Claire answered, avoiding the other woman's eyes. She wondered if Jess could tell what had happened to her. She felt exposed, naked, as if anyone must have been able to see at a glance that she was no longer what she had been yesterday.

She offered to sit with the sick mother and her babies, glad of an excuse to miss the departure of the yacht. But she could hear the shouts and singing of the islanders as they helped to haul the boat into the water, and the farewell song of the island chanted in perfect harmony signalled to her that the *Bella Donna* had finally left.

Jess had, surprisingly, kissed her good-bye and handed her a piece of paper with an address on it, saying, 'Write to me. Let me know how things go on.'

And she had promised, but later she screwed up the paper and threw it away. She wouldn't write, because she didn't want to keep in touch with anyone who had a connection with Scott. She intended to wipe all memories of him from her mind. And if it was humanly possible, she intended to be gone from the island before he returned.

That was easier than she had expected. Only three days later a helicopter landed carrying urgent supplies, including a portable tank and repair parts for the water-purification system, requested on their behalf by the captain of the *Bella Donna*. Then the sick mother and her babies were loaded on for the return trip; they were to be taken to a larger hospital with better facilities. When Claire asked if she could be the one to accompany them on the journey and keep an eye on them, Sister Amy at first looked doubtful, then said, 'Well, their condition is stable at the moment. If they should get worse on the way, you could probably do as much for them as any trained nurse. And if Sister Loretta or I were to go, goodness knows when we'd get back here, where we're needed. I'll give you all the instructions I can and . . . Very well, Claire. You go.'

'It need only be a one-way trip for me,' Claire said. 'I've almost finished my year here, and I could go straight on to Australia.'

'Yes, of course,' Sister Amy agreed serenely after

a moment's surprise. 'I don't suppose the children will mind the gap, and the Order is sending another teacher to replace you within a month or two.'

'I'll scarcely be missed,' Claire said, smiling bravely.

'Of course you'll be missed,' Sister Amy assured her warmly. 'That's the wonder of God's creation, that each of his children is unique. No person can truly replace another. We don't forget those who have touched our lives and entered our hearts.'

The words rang a knell in Claire's heart. There was one person she had to forget, one person who had entered her life unawares and taken possession without invitation. That was a memory that she was determined to exorcise.

Mother Josephine's welcome held a certain reserve. She accepted Claire's explanation for her early return with a hint of skepticism, but made no comment. 'Was the island climate hard on you?' she asked. 'You look tanned, but washed out.'

'I'm tired from travelling,' Claire said swiftly. 'And the hurricane was a strain, of course. We all lost some sleep.'

'Of course. And . . . you still want to join the order?'

'Yes.' Claire closed her eyes and reiterated fervently, 'Oh, please, yes, Reverend Mother.'

Mother Josephine smiled. 'Then, my dear, welcome. I'll ask the novice mistress to come and talk to you, and she will take you over to the postulants' quarters and give you a room.'

As the nun went to the door, Claire said hesitantly, 'Mother?'

'Yes?'

'Should I . . . If . . . a postulant feels that she is . . . unworthy . . .'

'I think we discussed that before, Claire. No one is worthy of Christ. We can only ask him to look with favour on our poor efforts.'

'I meant . . . if a novice felt that some specific . . . specific sin . . . made her ineligible . . .'

'Claire,' Mother Josephine said gently, 'has all our teaching been for nothing? There is no sin that God will not forgive if the person is truly repentant. You know that. The order does not demand perfection in its entrants, only the will to try to attain it.'

'I thought that perhaps I should tell you . . .' Her voice trailed off, her eyes fixed on her twisting hands.

After a moment the nun said, 'My dear, I am not a confessor. There is nothing you must tell me, unless you wish to.'

Her wise, troubled eyes rested on the bent fair head. Then Claire said quietly, 'No. Thank you, Mother.'

Claire gratefully accepted the routine of convent life, the early rising, the regular communal prayers, the periods of silence and meditation built around the daily work of the community in the school and children's home. Though the postulants were not admitted to the full routine of the nuns' lives and were asked to study a good deal in preparation for becoming novice sisters at the end of six months, the convent atmosphere pervaded the postulant quarters and, as the community was not large, the trainees and professed sisters had quite a lot of contact with one another. Claire found the quiet, contemplative times set aside for private prayer and meditation difficult, because they gave her too much time to think, and no matter how she tried to direct her thoughts to higher things, she found too often that her mind reverted to the very events she had hoped to wipe out of it forever.

She hadn't expected to see anyone from the island again, but when Claire was only a few months into her prenovitiate training, Sister Loretta was sent back to Australia to recuperate from a viral infection that had left her weak and in need of rest. She was staying with her family, but when she began to feel a little better she visited the convent to give the postulants and novices a short talk about the work of the mission. She told them also about the hurricane and its aftermath, and asked them to pray for the welfare of the islanders, who had now used up the food that the hurricane had left intact and were dependent on outside aid until their crops could be grown again.

'We have been fortunate in having one benefactor,' she added. 'A man who happened to be there when the hurricane struck.' She looked at Claire then, in the small audience, and said, 'You would remember Mr. Carver, Claire.'

Claire's eyes went wide, her face paling with shock.

Loretta looked at her curiously and went on. 'He's been back several times, bringing extra supplies and building materials. He even chartered a plane to send in food for us and the neighbouring islands. It seems we've only to mention that we're short of something, and he'll provide it.'

Afterwards the two of them took a stroll in the convent grounds, and Loretta said, 'You seemed . . . surprised when I mentioned Mr. Carver's help.'

'I didn't think he'd come back,' Claire said with difficulty.

'That's odd, because I gathered that he'd told you specifically that he would. He was quite upset, I think, to find you had gone while he was away. I'd almost say . . . angry.'

'He had no right to be angry. I didn't promise . . .'

Her voice trailed off in confusion, and for a few moments they strolled on in silence. Then, 'He gave me a message for you,' Loretta said. 'He made me promise to deliver it if I saw you.'

'I don't want to hear it,' Claire said swiftly.

Loretta hesitated. 'Are you sure?'

'Oh, please! I don't want to talk about him; I don't want to think about him!'

Loretta said gently, 'We can't help thinking about those we love, Claire.'

Claire stopped short, looking helplessly at her friend. 'Love?'

'That's what troubles you, isn't it?' Loretta asked.

'I don't love him. I'm going to be a nun.'

Slowly Loretta said, 'One doesn't necessarily cancel out the other. It's difficult, I know. But . . . love comes from God, Claire. One can . . . give it back to him.'

'I don't know what you mean.'

Loretta looked down at her clasped hands and suggested, 'Let's walk some more. I'm going to tell you something that may help.'

They strolled under tall old trees surrounded by

gardens that the nuns had lovingly tended since the founding of the convent more than a hundred years before. Loretta spoke quietly, her eyes on the landscape, her hands loosely clasped in front of her.

'I told you that I had always intended to be a nun, from when I was a child,' she said. 'And I told you that I was happy in my vocation. It was true, but there was a time . . . last year, when I almost gave it up. I realised that I was in love and, of course, that's something that isn't supposed to happen to a nun.'

'Father Damien,' Claire said with soft surprise.

'Yes. I suppose in a way it was inevitable. We were young, working together in a remote area with not much other company, and we shared so much—ideals, work, prayer. It . . . it hit me rather suddenly that I cared a great deal for him, and also that . . . that he cared for me. I think it would have been easier if it hadn't been for that. It sometimes seemed such a waste, you see.'

'Yes,' Claire agreed softly. 'Did you . . . did you tell him how you felt?'

Loretta smiled. 'Claire, he was the only priest on the island. He had to be my confessor.'

'Oh. Yes, of course.'

'At first, there was no other mention of it. But . . . there came a time when we had to talk about it together, outside the confessional. As a man and a woman with a . . . a mutual problem.'

'And?'

Loretta drew a deep breath. 'And we discussed the whole thing, with all its implications. We loved each other, but both of us had deliberately chosen—and promised ourselves to—a way of life that precluded marriage and children and physical love. We had to decide whether we had perhaps chosen wrongly, after all . . . that our vocations were mistaken. Or whether we simply weren't strong enough to carry them out. We might have applied for dispensation from our vows, and if that was granted, we would have been free to marry. Of course, you know it's being done quite often now. One of the girls who was professed with me has left the convent and married. She's quite sure that she did the right thing. It was a very tempting prospect for Damien and me. And for a while we became quite excited by it. We wanted'—her voice shook a little—'we wanted very badly to be together.'

'Are you . . . going to?' Claire asked.

'Well, we decided not to do anything in haste. We gave ourselves time to pray about it, and think, and then we talked some more.'

She stopped and reached out a hand, picking a leaf at random from a nearby eucalyptus. The sun shone through its branches, dappling her nun's veil as she turned the leaf in her fingers. 'I thought about it really deeply,' she said. 'I was awfully young when I made up my mind, as you know. Perhaps I was influenced by a sort of hero worship of my older sister and my family's enthusiasm for the idea. But I had never doubted before. I've been very happy in religious life. Very close to God. I would hate to lose that. And I had not given my vows lightly. By the time I made my final profession, I knew absolutely clearly what I was doing, I thought. Although I . . . had not experienced the full power of love for a man. Of course I had my crushes on boys as a teenager, times when I thought I might give up the idea of the convent, after all. But always I felt that

God's call was there, and that his love was stronger, much stronger, than any love I could find in the world. I found it easy to give up my youthful loves for him. I thought I was being strong, then. . . .'

She looked up, her eyes shining with humour. Claire prompted involuntarily, 'And now?'

The laughter faded. 'Now it's much harder. Now I'm a woman, not a teenage girl. This time I really know what it is I'm giving up.'

'Giving up?'

'Yes. Oddly enough, we both came to the same decision in the end. We love each other, and we won't deny that. It's a gift for which we can't be other than grateful, although at times it's a painful one. But we love our vows, our commitment to the religious life, even more. That takes precedence for us both. We want very much to stand by our promises to God. We went through a difficult time for a few months, but in a strange way our love for each other has lent us strength. We don't see each other alone, of course, unless it's absolutely necessary. I've asked to be transferred away from the island, and now, because of my health, I expect I'll be sent somewhere else. I sometimes think that God sent me that illness in his mercy, to answer my prayers for his help.'

'You'll miss the island.'

'Yes. But it will be easier for Damien.'

'And you?'

'In some ways, yes. The thing is, Claire, I'm sure God doesn't expect us to repudiate our love, or try to pretend it doesn't exist. It does, and it's good. What we do about it . . . that's the important thing. It can enrich our lives and be freely given back to

God, who gave it to us. Oh, we might have chosen differently; some people do. But that's for them to decide, with God's help. Each person is different, with a different destiny within the Divine Plan. But I'm sure, and so is Damien, that this way is right for us. We're happy with our decision.'

Claire looked at Loretta's face, saw the slight sadness in her eyes, but also the serenity that overlaid it, and envied her. 'I believe you,' she said.

Loretta laughed a little. 'I started to tell you this because I thought it might help you,' she said. 'I seem to have ended up pouring out my heart.'

'I don't love Scott Carver,' Claire said. 'The problem is . . . I think I hate him.'

Loretta frowned. 'What has he done to deserve it?'

Claire shook her head. 'I don't want to talk about it.'

'If that's how you feel . . . He told me to tell you where to find him if you need him. "If she needs me." That's what he said.'

'I don't want to know!' Claire said fiercely. 'I mean it!'

Loretta touched her arm gently. 'Then I won't go on. But . . . Claire, hatred won't help you.'

'I know,' Claire said tiredly. 'I know.'

Claire had another visitor sometime later, this one totally unexpected. She was called to Mother Josephine's office one day and found the superior looking less than calm. 'There is someone waiting to see you, Claire. It . . . it may be something of a shock.'

Claire went white. 'Scott . . . ?' she whispered.

Mother Josephine's eyes flickered curiously over

her. 'No, that isn't his name. It's . . . Mr. Pietro Benotti.'

Claire stared back, her heart beginning a peculiarly loud, slow thumping. Then she jerkily shook her head. 'I don't think I want to see him,' she said, her voice thin and high.

'I think that you should,' Mother Josephine said, her eyes compassionate but her mouth firm. 'He has asked to be allowed to . . . to tell you something. It's important.'

The man who turned from his contemplation of the garden when she entered the visitors' parlour and quietly closed the door was tall and dark, with silver lights in his black hair. When he faced her, she could see that he was still handsome, though his expression held a grimness that could have been frightening.

Then he smiled, and the grimness gave way to a stunning charm. 'Claire?' he said, and started forward, his arms outstretched as though to embrace her.

Startled, Claire took an automatic step backwards, and he stopped, letting his hands fall to his sides and shrugging ruefully in a very Italian way, although his accent when he spoke again was barely noticeable. 'Forgive me,' he said. 'I have been thinking of you so much that I feel I know you, but you . . .'

He looked suddenly at a loss, pushing his fingers through his thick hair, although she was convinced that he was a man who was seldom confounded. 'It's difficult,' he confessed. 'For you, too, I suppose. You do know who I am?'

Finding her voice, she said, 'Yes. My mother's husband.'

'That's correct.' He shoved his hands into his pockets suddenly and stared down at the worn carpet. 'I came to see you,' he said, 'for several reasons. Some will take much explaining, I'm afraid. But I must first tell you that . . .' He looked up at her, and in his eyes she saw pain, and something told her what was to come. '. . . that your mother is dead,' he finished quietly.

He watched her, his face grim again, but his eyes softening the expression, because they were full of concern. 'I'm sorry if it's a shock,' he said. 'I wanted to tell you myself. I feel that I . . . that we owe you that much, at least.'

She didn't know what to say. She felt quite remote from the scene, as if it was being played by someone else while she watched from the sidelines. Her mother was dead, but her mother had been dead to her for years, and her one attempt to resurrect the relationship had been a dismaying failure. She ought to feel grief, or at least pity . . . something, instead of this disconcerting numbness.

He was waiting for her to react, to say something, and she walked jerkily forward, clutching at the back of a chair. 'I . . . haven't seen my mother for a long time,' she said. 'Was she ill? She died recently?'

'Quite recently,' he answered. 'A matter of a few weeks only. Forgive me, but I could not ask you to come . . . to attend the funeral. You see,' he explained carefully, 'I did not, until a few days ago, know of your existence.'

She managed to smile at him faintly, understanding his embarrassment. 'No,' she said. 'I realise that, Mr. Benotti.'

He moved suddenly, some of the anguish he must have felt showing in his agitated hands, his face. 'I found a letter from the convent in her papers after she died,' he said. 'I couldn't believe it, at first, that she could keep such a thing from me. I checked with the convent immediately and was told that Gail did have a daughter who had been left here as a child, and that . . . soon after she married me, she ceased visiting her little girl. I found it difficult to believe, to accept. My wife never mentioned you. I cannot criticise her; I loved her, but this . . .' He gestured, conveying a sort of helpless anger. '. . . this was unforgivable. I have a stepdaughter, and I've been unaware of the fact. It isn't easy to realise. . . .'

'It's all right, Mr. Benotti; I have no claim on you. And I don't blame you for what my mother did.'

He looked, for a moment, very angry, and she thought that her mother might well have had reason to be afraid of his temper. Harshly he said, 'I'm not worried about any claims you may have or not have. When I first found out about you it was my wish to take you into my home, to try to make up to you for the years when I knew nothing of you. To atone for your mother's . . . abandonment. I'm afraid that you have cause to blame her very much. She was not always wise. In many ways she was childlike; she would always put off unpleasantness for as long as possible. She lived for the day. It was charming . . . and exasperating. But what she did to you—that was . . . I can only say, she cannot have realised . . . I hope you can find it in your heart to forgive her.'

Claire didn't know at that moment whether that was possible. She bowed her head silently.

He went on, his voice becoming very gentle. 'It was easier to find you than I thought. I had not expected you to be a novice in the very convent where you were brought up.'

'I'm only a postulant,' she explained. 'I hope to start my novitiate in a few months' time.'

'You do intend to go on with it? It is what you truly want?'

'It's what I truly want.'

He sighed, sounding rather frustrated, then shrugged, looking around the small, bare parlour and then back at her. 'If you are happy here I won't insist on removing you. But . . . my home is yours, Claire, if you should wish it. I hope you will not mind that I say, with all humility, that I would like to be regarded as your father.'

Suddenly, unexpectedly, her eyes filled with tears. The invitation, so long awaited and long ago despaired of, and given now with such sincerity and generosity, overwhelmed her.

He made a soft exclamation and closed the space between them to take her in his arms, patting her shoulder as she let the tears fall on his beautifully cut jacket and lending her his handkerchief when she drew away from him at last, apologising.

'Don't be sorry,' he said gravely. 'I'm your papa. I never had a daughter, you know. Only sons. It's been a sorrow to me, but now . . . Claire, are you really quite sure you wish to be a nun?'

Claire nodded.

'Well, it's a noble and holy thing, and I should not mind giving a daughter to the Church. But it's hard, when I have only just discovered that daughter. I had made such plans for you. . . . But never mind. Only promise me one thing.'

'If I can.'

'If you change your mind and want to leave the convent after all, come to me. Let me get to know the daughter I was denied for so long.'

His dark eyes were gentle and pleading, and she said, 'Yes. I promise. But—'

He held up his hand. 'I know, I know. You are determined to stay here. Well, I wish you well, whatever you do. May I come and visit you again?'

'Of course. With Reverend Mother's permission. Do . . . your sons . . . know about me?'

His smile flashed again. 'Your brothers?'

Her heart warmed to him again at his ready acceptance of the relationship. 'My brothers,' she said shyly.

'I've not told them yet,' he admitted. 'I was a little afraid that you might not want to have anything to do with us. I wouldn't have them disappointed. Would you like to meet them?'

'Very much,' she said. 'But . . .'

'But?' he queried, frowning.

'I don't know . . .' She faltered. She was truthfully a little afraid, a little nervous of this new twist her life had taken. 'I feel rather unsettled by all this. Let me get used to it first.'

'Of course. I won't tell them just yet. Perhaps soon, hmm?'

'Perhaps.'

She remembered her mother promising her that soon she would introduce her to her stepfather, soon she would be taken to live with them. Her mouth trembled unexpectedly, and Pietro Benotti put a strong, warm hand over hers. 'What is it?'

She shook her head. 'You will come back, won't you?' she asked.

'Of course. I will give you my address,' he said, sliding a hand into his breast pocket. 'You are permitted to write to your family?'

Her family. The words had a comforting sound.

'Yes,' she said. 'Have you come specially from Adelaide?'

'No, we're back in Sydney now. We came here just before your mother became ill,' he said, and then stared at her. 'You knew that we lived in Adelaide?'

She flushed under his keen gaze. 'I . . . I heard that you did,' she said. 'You're quite well known.'

He shrugged. 'No, I'm not. Only to people in my line of business. How did you hear? You never tried to find us.'

She looked away, twisting her hands nervously together.

'Claire?' He put a gentle finger under her chin and made her look at him. 'Why didn't you contact us?'

Sister Josephine had not told him, obviously, about her abortive attempt to do so almost two years ago.

Tongue-tied, she stared back at him in silence. 'You tried?' he said at last, his eyes piercing.

This was the man for whom her mother had abandoned her, the man who had loved Gail despite her childlike lack of responsibility, and who had forgiven his dead wife for depriving him of a daughter he might also have loved. Now she could tell him of Gail's heartless second rejection of her. It might shatter the last of his illusions about his dead wife and show her up for what she really was, selfish, shallow and hard. This was her opportunity for revenge on her mother.

In an instant, she knew she couldn't do it. She met his eyes, her own clear and steady, and said, 'I thought about it. But I decided that it might be better not to. You might not have wanted me, after all.'

The stern suspicion in his eyes melted. 'You are wanted,' he assured her. 'I suppose that, as time passed, Gail must have put off telling me about you until one day it was too late. She was, I'm afraid, like that. None of us is perfect. But, Claire, if only you had written to her, contacted her, when you were older, I'm certain she would have plucked up the courage to tell me. She would have welcomed you, as I do.'

Claire nodded and managed to smile at him. 'Thank you. Perhaps she would have.'

'Of course. Believe me.'

'Yes. I believe you.' Technically, of course, it was a lie, but she placated her conscience with the charity of the act. Hadn't St. Paul, that sternest of moralists, put charity at the head of all the virtues?

Chapter Eight

After six months as postulants the girls who had asked to enter the order were preparing to enter the next stage—the novitiate. As novices they would begin to adopt the normal routine of the order's life and take more part in its work of teaching and nursing along with the professed sisters. Part of the preparation for the 'clothing' ceremony which signified their formal entry into the novitiate was a 'retreat' during which extra periods of silence and prayer were observed, and a priest came each day to give them lectures on the spiritual life and prepare them for meditations on religious themes.

The ritual of the clothing was an important one. The girls would approach the altar dressed symbolically in white bridal gowns to show that they would accept no earthly love, only the love of God himself, dedicating themselves to him forever. After formally declaring their intentions they would be blessed by the bishop and given their novices' habits and veils, then set about learning in earnest to be sisters of the Order.

Five days into the retreat, Claire fainted in the refectory one morning as grace was being said at breakfast.

She recovered quite quickly, but the novice mistress insisted on her being taken to the infirmary and, in spite of Claire's protests, called in a doctor to examine her.

Later she was allowed to return to the routine of the retreat, but in the afternoon Mother Josephine sent for her.

'I have been talking with Sister Anne,' Mother Josephine began, after Claire had seated herself. 'The doctor has expressed some concern about you.'

'I only fainted. It's nothing.'

'The reason for your fainting concerns me, Claire. I have noticed, of course, that you appear to be losing weight, and Sister Anne has mentioned to me that you've developed migraine headaches several times lately, and that she's sent you off to rest.'

'They're not usually that bad. . . .'

'You mean that you've had others, not severe enough for Sister Anne to have noticed?'

Claire mumbled, 'I expect they're only ordinary headaches, not migraines.'

'They appear to have the classic symptoms. You've been covering them up, haven't you? Carrying on as though nothing was wrong? Have you taken anything for them?'

Claire shook her head.

'And now the doctor tells us that you've been starving yourself, as well.'

'Oh, I haven't! I eat—'

'Very little. And hardly any protein. Our diet, Claire, isn't rich, but it *is* designed to maintain health. You're apparently suffering from anemia, or so the doctor suspects. I think,' Mother Josephine went on sternly, 'that you have been fasting, and fasting to excess. Prayer and penance are contained in the Rule, Claire, but no sister is permitted to abuse her body to the point of making herself ill. It might have done in the Middle Ages, but it is not now considered a sign of holiness to despise the body which was given to you by God. One should respect his creation.'

'Yes, I know,' Claire acknowledged humbly. 'I'm sorry. I didn't mean to make myself sick.'

'Well, please eat sensibly in future. And the doctor has prescribed iron pills, which you will take, and advice for the migraines, which you will also follow. Is that understood?'

'Yes, Mother.'

She stirred as if ready to leave, but Mother Josephine said, 'Don't go yet. I want to talk to you. I don't feel that we've reached the bottom of this.' For a few seconds she looked down at the desk before her, apparently marshalling her thoughts. Then she said kindly, 'For some reason you have a need to punish yourself, Claire. What makes you feel so guilty? Is it something to do with your mother's death? Do you still feel that you hate her? Is that it?'

'No. I don't hate her anymore. I feel rather sorry for her. My . . . stepfather may not realise what a formidable man he is, and he loved her, so he doesn't understand why she should have been afraid of him. But I think she was. I think she just wasn't brave enough to confess a past mistake to him, and I suppose, if she'd been let down once, as she must have been by my father, she didn't trust her new husband's love enough to risk its happening again.'

'That's a very mature and understanding assessment,' Mother Josephine commented. 'So if it isn't that, would you like to tell me what the problem is?'

'You said once that you're not a confessor.'

Mother Josephine looked down at her hands. 'No. Well, if it's a problem that you prefer to confide in your confessor, that is of course your privilege and I won't press it. But there is one thing I would like to say to you. I hope that you are taking the opportunity given you by this special period of prayer and preparation to rigorously assess your suitability for religious life. That is what the long training is for, and especially these retreats before important steps toward the final vows, so that you can be quite sure before you commit yourself irrevocably that this is really what you are suited for, and what God requires of you in this life.'

'You don't . . . think that I'm suitable?' Claire murmured.

Sister Josephine smiled understandingly. 'My dear, do you remember the seven deadly sins? They're not much spoken of these days, and many of them are no longer considered so deadly. They were originally written down for those in monastic life, did you know that?'

Claire shook her head.

'One of them is sloth.' She held up a hand as Claire moved sharply, ready to protest. 'No, I'm not accusing you of laziness. You err rather on the side of too much zeal. But perhaps for the wrong things. You see, like many words, sloth has changed its meaning. It originally meant a kind of refusal of joy, a dull and subdued, rigidly rule-bound approach to life, especially to monastic life. I've watched you a great deal, Claire, since you came back to us. I see hard work and dedication and a will to suffer if necessary to succeed at what you've chosen to do. I see no joy.'

Joy. The face that came to mind was Loretta's when she spoke about her love for Damien, and her even greater love for the way of life she had chosen. There had been sadness in her eyes, but, contradictorily, there had also been a kind of serene joy.

Claire said, 'I feel that I don't deserve it.'

Mother Josephine was unsurprised. 'Yes. You seem to me to be shutting yourself off from life, from any kind of pleasure in it. You are not silly enough to believe that all pleasure in life and what it offers us is sinful. Something has happened to you, I know. Something that has plunged you back into that misery of abandonment that you experienced as a small child. You must never feel that God has abandoned you, my dear. He will not do that. The greatest sin we can commit is to despair of his love and his mercy. Whatever this terrible burden of guilt is about,' she said, 'you have presumably confessed it in the Sacrament of Reconciliation?'

'Yes, of course.'

'And the priest believed in your true contrition and absolved you?'

'Yes.'

'Claire, we believe that Christ gave his priests

power to forgive sin in his name, that when a priest gives absolution and the penitent is truly sorry, God himself has extended his full pardon and reconciled you to him. Who are you to withhold from yourself a forgiveness which God has extended to you without reservation? He has given you the right to joy, but you alone have the means to obtain it.'

'You mean, through the religious life?'

'If that's the right life for you. There are other paths to God, some of them less direct, but they're no less valuable if they're the right paths in his sight. We both know that priests and nuns are regarded with special respect in the church, that often it's been said that the religious life is the better way. But it's only better for those who are called to it.'

'You're still not sure that *I'm* called to it, are you?'

'No. I'm not sure. But I'm not sure that you're *not* called to it, either.'

'I . . . If I told you that . . . someone said I have a great capacity for passion . . . do you think that would indicate that I'm not . . . not suited to the religious life?'

The nun's brows rose slightly. 'No, not necessarily. I believe that the life of a nun is very suitable for girls who have a great capacity for passion, and a great capacity for directing it to the service of God.'

'I meant . . .' Claire floundered, her cheeks hot, and Mother Josephine gave her an amused smile, the skin around her eyes crinkling with laughter. 'I know exactly what you meant, my dear. Have you ever seen a picture of Bernini's sculpture of *Saint Teresa of Avila in Ecstasy?*'

Claire shook her head. 'I don't think so.'

'There must be one in the convent library somewhere. Try to find it later. Teresa the Great was a very practical and highly intelligent woman, not given to flights of fancy and not in the least neurotic. But she was a mystic, too. She was also capable of great passion, which she put at the service of God and the Carmelite Order. At one time she described a vision of heavenly joy which was granted to her while praying. Bernini translated her description, which was extremely vivid, into his sculpture.'

Mother Josephine paused and continued rather dryly, 'In this post-Freudian age some observers have made remarks about the sculpture which they imagine to be rather daring and even blasphemous. Of course, Bernini was rendering a spiritual experience in material terms, and he was not present when Teresa's mystical vision took place. He portrayed a woman in ecstasy . . . of the only sort he knew.'

Claire sat very still, a little puzzled, but listening carefully.

Mother Josephine went on, 'Some pious people are embarrassed by Bernini's Teresa. They find the portrayal of spiritual passion in unmistakably physical form unacceptable. But both kinds of passion are God's gifts to humanity. Two sides of the same coin, one might say. And being capable of one does not preclude the other. Perhaps *cannot* preclude the other. Saint Thomas Aquinas, the great theologian, said that the physical expression of sexual love gives glory to God, and that the pleasure of the lovers increases its moral goodness.'

Claire looked up. 'Did he?'

Mother Josephine smiled, nodding.

'But not . . . sex outside marriage,' Claire said flatly. 'Then . . . it's wrong.'

'The church has always taught that sexual love belongs within marriage, certainly. But, ultimately, only God can say to what extent it is sinful for a person to use one of His gifts in a wrong context. Something which is in itself good—as sexual passion is—surely cannot be made wholly bad, unless the person engaging in it is consciously and deliberately subverting the act to evil intentions. Remember, Claire, it's really quite difficult for people to commit a *mortal* sin and cut themselves off entirely from God's grace.'

Claire smiled slightly. 'I remember,' she said. 'You always told us that. One must know exactly how serious it is and really have the will to do wrong.'

'And the act itself must be gravely sinful,' Mother Josephine finished. 'You've retained some of what I taught you, then.'

'A lot. You always had a knack of stating things very clearly.'

'Thank you. I have a feeling you've been somewhat muddled, lately.'

'Yes, I have. I feel a little better now.'

'That's good.' The nun smiled at her affectionately. 'Leave yourself open to joy, Claire. Let God do the rest.'

She did not achieve joy, but she did manage to reach a hard-won decision. The filmy white dress and veil that hung in her small, plain room, which Sister Anne in traditional phrasing still referred to as her 'cell,' drew her eyes each time she entered. She had thought that when the time came to make her first tentative promises to God, to give him her love exclusively for life, she would be filled with ardent happiness. But as the time grew nearer she found instead that she was more and more often assailed by feelings of dread, of guilt, and most of all by a dark conviction of wrongness.

In the end, although something inside her wept for what might have been, she went to Mother Josephine and admitted that she could not go through with the ceremony, that she knew the religious life was not, after all, for her. She cried a little, accepted the comfort of Mother Josephine's arms and tried to believe the superior's assurance that her leaving was not an admission of failure but a realistic decision and the start of a new direction for her.

'I seem to have gone in so many directions,' she sighed dejectedly. 'I don't even know what I'm going to do.'

'Your stepfather . . . ?' Mother Josephine suggested tentatively.

'Yes. I must tell him. He made me promise to go to him if I ever changed my mind about the convent.'

'Then do that, my dear. He's a good man, I think. You haven't met your brothers, have you?'

'No. He wanted to bring them to visit, and I know he asked you if there would be any objection. He told me you said it was all right. But I . . . couldn't. I think perhaps I've been afraid. Afraid that a family would distract me from what I wanted to do.'

'I feel that all your life you've had a great longing for a family, haven't you, Claire?'

'Perhaps, deep down.'

'I've always thought that you ought to be married

and have children. I've watched you with the children here and I suspect that, for you, other people's children are not enough.'

'I have sometimes thought . . . that it would be nice.'

'My dear girl, you've sometimes thought that you couldn't bear not to have babies of your own. I've seen it in your face.'

'You know a lot about me.'

'Not everything. But I think that you have a great store of love dammed up inside you, and that it's been starved of suitable human objects. It's all very well to give all one's love to God. But human beings learn about love through human relationships. Christ made it quite clear that one cannot love God and not love other people. You missed out on a close, complete family as a child, and were deprived too soon of having one person to love above all others. People who have been brought up in a loving family may be able to spread their love widely when they grow up, and may not need, in human terms, that narrow focus. Your life has been different. I think perhaps you will only fully experience love when you find a man you want to marry. Don't be afraid of its taking you away from God, Claire. Real, mature love for another person can only bring you closer to Him who *is* love.'

Her stepfather's home was a stunning contrast to the austerity of the convent. Located in North Sydney, overlooking Lavender Bay and the harbour, it was in a new high-rise block of spacious luxury apartments.

She was given her own room with a view of the

water from her window which opened onto a private balcony, and told to consider the place her home from then on.

Rather apprehensive about meeting her half-brothers, she was warmed and relieved when Paul, the younger of the two, and Jonnie, christened Giovanni, welcomed her with grins and hugs, as well as a frank and disarming curiosity. They were handsome boys, taking after their father, both tall and dark, with brilliant brown eyes and breathtaking smiles.

'You don't look like our sister!' Paul told her the first evening as he caught a glimpse of both her and himself in the ornate mirror on the wall of the apartment.

'She is like her mother—your mother,' Pietro said swiftly. 'Beautiful.'

Claire shook her head, her mouth curving skeptically. She could scarcely remember what her mother had looked like, and she gazed with great interest at a photographic portrait of Gail that hung in the large lounge. It showed a woman who was blond and conventionally pretty, beautifully made up and smiling just enough to show perfect teeth and a lovely mouth. It looked posed and gave nothing away about the personality behind the face.

'She did not photograph well,' Pietro said, coming up behind her as she studied the photograph. 'She was at her best when she was animated—laughing, talking. Then she was irresistible.'

She looked at the longing and the grief in his face, and was struck again by the fact of his love for her mother, wondering how a strong, sensitive man like him could have fallen so heavily for a woman who had given every evidence of being vain, immature and self-centred. Somewhere in her he had found something that no one else had been able to tap. Perhaps something that her mother had suppressed in the bitter aftermath of her disastrous love affair and in the necessity of caring for the baby that had resulted from it, until Pietro had come along and with his love unlocked some hidden wellspring of generosity and love in return.

She wanted to find a job immediately, but Pietro vetoed the idea, insisting that she was too thin, needed a period of rest and pampering, and then . . . 'After a month or two, we will see,' he said.

Perhaps he hoped she would get used to the life of a spoiled daughter which he seemed determined to foist on her and forget about earning a living. He wanted to take care of her, but at first she wouldn't allow it. Then, as she saw him begin to get angry over the issue, she temporarily gave in. He was unused to having his will crossed, but she hoped that soon he would tire of his doting-father role and realise that she was an adult, with a life of her own.

Having a daughter was a new and pleasurable experience for him, and he intended to enjoy it to the full. He showered presents and new clothes on her, and when she protested, the boys added their persuasions to his, not showing the least signs of jealousy. All three of them would advise her on her clothes and comment on her looks with frank Italian admiration. She suspected that they all thought of her as some new kind of animated toy, but she hoped that when the novelty of her presence in their lives wore off, they would be less protective and possessive of her and adopt a more casual attitude.

Meantime, it was a welcome change, she had to admit to herself, to live a life of the purest pleasure. Her hair had grown until it just touched her shoulders, swinging in a smooth bell, and she began to use makeup that discreetly highlighted her colouring and to choose clothes that were becoming as well as modest.

Pietro introduced her to several blatantly eligible men, up-and-coming executives and bright young tycoons. She went out with some of them, mainly because Pietro obviously wanted her to, but also because she hoped that one day she might meet a man who would attract her as much as Scott Carver had done, and who also shared some of her own values.

One of the men she liked was not directly involved in business. He was Gareth Seymour, a lawyer who had helped in arranging some contracts for Pietro and was invited round for a celebratory drink afterwards. He was thirtyish, quiet and clever, with the kind of smooth looks which were nondescript at first sight, but which, Claire soon noted, included keenly observant eyes and an attractive masculine grace and economy of movement. She wasn't surprised to find on their first date that he was an excellent dancer, and although she hadn't had much practice, he soon brought out her own latent sense of rhythm and taught her to enjoy dancing, too.

Gareth took her out several times, and Claire was aware that Pietro was watching the progress of the relationship with hawklike interest, while Paul and

Jonnie took every opportunity to indulge themselves in the delightful new pastime of brotherly teasing.

'We're only friends,' she told them firmly. 'Gareth is a nice man and I enjoy his company.'

It was almost true, but not quite. Gareth's company was pleasant, and she was sure he was a nice man. None of the escorts Pietro had introduced to her had made any kind of persistent advances, and she inferred that her stepfather had subtly conveyed that he expected his 'daughter' to be respected. Gareth, she felt, was not the type to be intimidated. He was just naturally courteous and not a man likely to treat a woman like prey. But her interest had quickened the first time he kissed her, deliberately and with some expertise, gently but firmly overriding her initial slight resistance and making sure that she enjoyed the experience.

The enjoyment was new to her. She had been kissed several times by other men since leaving the convent, sometimes with her cooperation, sometimes not. The most she could say of any of the kisses was that they hadn't been unpleasant. For the first time since the night on the island with Scott, she felt a stirring of sensual pleasure when Gareth took her in his arms.

Cautiously, she withheld any response, and when he released her and regarded her quizzically, a finger softly tracing the outline of her lips, she lowered her eyelids so as not to meet his gaze.

'You've got a gorgeous mouth,' he said. 'Forgive me?'

Her eyelids flickered up for a moment. 'There's nothing to forgive. Thank you for a lovely evening.'

His hand fell away. He said mildly, 'I wasn't claiming payment, you know.'

'No,' she said. 'I didn't mean to imply that.'

'Care to repeat the experience?'

She looked up quickly, and he laughed and said, 'The evening out. There's a rather good concert at the opera house next week. Will you come with me? We could have dinner first.'

She acquiesced, and accepted his good-night kiss afterwards, curious to know if the pleasurable sensation would be repeated. When it was, she felt an odd satisfaction. Although it was nothing like the fury of desire that Scott had aroused in her, at least it proved that she was capable of some kind of sexual response to another man.

They were dining out one night in a quaint new restaurant at the Rocks, an area once the notorious haunt of ex-convicts and now refurbished, when she noticed something familiar about a dark-haired woman at a nearby table where a party of four was sitting.

At the same time the young woman looked up and saw Claire, and her rather bored expression turned into a brilliant, pleased and disbelieving smile.

If Claire had kept the instinctive glow of recognition from her own face, Jess might have thought she had made a mistake, but now it was too late. Excusing herself to her companions, Jess came over, her hands outstretched, so that Claire was obliged to take them. 'Claire!' Jess's green eyes, alight with curiosity, passed over the deep red chiffon dress with the scoop neckline and noted the longer hair, the lip gloss and eye shadow. She laughed and said, 'Changed your mind?'

Claire nodded.

Jess, obviously wondering how much Gareth knew of Claire's past ambitions, flicked a glance at him as he stood up politely and indicated his chair, murmuring, 'Please sit down.'

Claire introduced them, and Gareth took an empty chair from another table and reseated himself.

'You didn't write to me!' Jess chided.

'I'm sorry. I . . . lost your address.'

'What are you doing now?' Again she shot a briefly curious look at Gareth, who stared back impassively.

'I'm living with my stepfather,' Claire said. 'It's a long story.'

Jess put a hand over hers briefly. 'I'd love to hear it,' she said. 'We're friends, aren't we . . . still?'

'Of course,' Claire said.

'I'll give you my address and phone number. Oh . . . I've left my bag . . .' She gestured vaguely in the direction of her table.

'I think I've got a pencil . . .' Claire started to say, but as she picked up her slim evening purse from the table she saw that Gareth was already offering Jess a small, elegant diary with a gold-topped pencil tucked into the spine.

'Help yourself to a page,' he said.

'Oh . . . thanks.' Jess barely glanced at him, just scribbled on one of the pages and tore it out to hand to Claire. 'Your turn,' she said, handing the book and pencil over, too. 'Give me your address.'

Claire looked to Gareth for permission and he

shrugged, then returned his gaze, rather enigmatically, to Jess. She was watching Claire write down her stepfather's address and telephone number, and stretched out a hand for the paper as Claire carefully tore out the page.

'I'd best get back,' she said with a slight grimace, 'and leave you to your escort.' Her eyes seemed to pass over Gareth, and her mouth curved in a polite little smile. 'Thanks,' she said carelessly. 'You can have your chair and your book back now . . . and your girl. See you, Claire. Lovely finding you again.'

After Jess had returned to her own table, Gareth said quietly, 'You didn't lose her address, did you?'

Claire looked up at him. 'What makes you say that?'

'You're not a good liar, and I'm trained to spot lies, remember? Why didn't you want to contact her?'

'Has my father told you that I had intended to be a nun?'

'Yes. He mentioned it.'

'Well, it's a little difficult to keep up outside friendships when you're in a convent. And not encouraged.'

He looked at her thoughtfully, as if he knew there was more to it, but didn't comment. Instead, he glanced over at the other table and said, 'Your friend doesn't seem to be enjoying herself much. Does she always look so bored?'

Following his gaze, she saw that Jess was leaning back slightly in her chair, holding a glass of wine in two hands and turning it idly, her eyes half-closed, while her three companions talked and laughed.

'Perhaps it's a defence,' Claire said softly.

She didn't think he heard her, because at that moment Jess looked up, straight into his eyes. Glancing at him, Claire saw that Gareth's face remained perfectly impassive, but he didn't look away as a person caught staring usually does, and his hand, which was loosely curved about his own wineglass, tightened and moved the glass a little, so that the liquid shivered and danced.

She looked back at Jess and saw the other girl's eyebrows rise a fraction in brief cynical surprise before she shifted her gaze to Claire and smiled at her.

'She's not a bad-looking bird when she smiles,' Gareth drawled, and Claire looked at him with slight shock. She had not heard that rather disparaging tone from him before.

'She's very attractive,' she protested. 'Don't you like her?'

He met her eyes, and she knew that something had angered him. But he smiled at her and shrugged. 'I've only exchanged two words with the lady.' He paused and added, 'I dislike arrogance in women.'

Claire blinked in surprise. He laughed softly, looking down at the table, and then into her eyes, his own rueful. 'All right, I suppose the truth is that she looked right through me, and my male pride couldn't stand it. Which is ridiculous, because everyone looks through me on first sight. It's a professional asset.'

Intrigued, and not quite sure how serious he was, Claire smiled a little uncertainly. 'She was surprised to see me; I'm sure she didn't mean to be rude.'

'Oh, she wasn't rude. Just politely dismissing.'

Claire laughed. 'Yes, I can see how that could be galling.'

'You can laugh.' He smiled at her. 'It isn't something that happens to beautiful women.'

She shook her head and finished her wine. Neither of them wanted coffee, and they left shortly afterwards.

'You're not serious about that man you were with the other night, are you?' Jess asked her when they met for lunch a few days later.

'Why?' Claire asked warily.

'He has cold eyes,' Jess said flatly. 'What is he, a prosecution lawyer?'

Claire laughed. 'You're close. He *is* a lawyer, but I don't think he's much involved in court work. He deals with contracts.'

'Oh yes? Mmm, that's probably more up his alley. Figures and paperwork, not people.'

'He's actually rather nice,' Claire said.

Jess regarded her interestedly. 'Is that your considered opinion?'

'Yes, it is.'

Suddenly Jess laughed, low and throaty. 'The poor man! Is he in love with you?'

'I don't know,' Claire said. 'I don't think so.'

'For his sake, I hope not!' But there was an odd inflection in her voice. 'I don't suppose there's any worse fate for a man than to be thought "rather nice." Talk about damning with faint praise!'

'Oh, Jess.' Claire smiled, biting her lip. 'You're incorrigible!'

'You're not in love with him, my sweet,' Jess said,

her eyes becoming keen suddenly. 'Are you—with anyone?'

Claire shook her head. 'I only left the convent a couple of months ago,' she said.

'Tell me about it?' Jess invited as the waitress brought their meals.

While they ate, Claire detailed the events of the past months, leaving out the reasons for her decision and dwelling on her stepfather's fortuitous entry into her life. She thought that Jess wasn't fooled, but was tactfully prepared to forgo awkward questions and follow the red herring of Claire's rediscovered family.

'Your stepfather sounds a perfect honey,' she remarked.

Claire laughed. 'Oh, I'm not sure if that's an apt description. He's rather formidable. Most people seem slightly scared of him.'

'Are *you?*'

'No. Well . . . a little nervous of him, perhaps. I really intend to talk to him about getting a job and earning my living, but I've kept putting it off because I know he doesn't want me to just yet. But he's always extraordinarily kind to me.'

'You're not a hard person to be kind to, Claire.' For a moment her expression softened. Then, with a touch of teasing she added, 'You bring out the best in people. Even me.'

Embarrassed, Claire said, 'It's nice of you to think so. But I don't know why you should speak of yourself in that way. You're really . . .'

'Rather nice?' Jess suggested dryly. 'Don't you dare!'

Claire laughed and changed the subject. Longing and yet dreading to hear about Scott, she asked instead, 'What happened to Felix?'

There was an odd pause.

'Felix,' Jess said, a strange, bitter little smile hovering about her mouth. 'Would you believe it? I actually showed some judgment, not to mention willpower, with Felix. He made a proposition . . . and I turned him down. Flat.'

'I think you did the right thing,' Claire said softly. 'But . . . it hurt, didn't it?'

'Isn't that silly?' Jess said, her voice deliberately light. 'Felix is a one-hundred-percent dyed-in-the-wool heartbreaker. I'm really pleased with myself that I managed to keep out of his clutches. But yes, it hurt. I tell you, I'm a crazy woman.'

'Not really.'

'No, not so crazy that I don't know I'd be hurt even more if I gave in to him. One thing, he never knew how I really felt. He said we were two of a kind, we could have a lot of good times. Well, I guess he was right. We could have. And he never would have known how I dreaded what was to come after the good times. I'd have been good old Jess, right to the end, when he dumped me for someone else. Well, I got out of that one.'

'And there's been no one else?'

Jess looked at her, her mouth twisting in a cynical smile. 'There've been several someone elses. None that mattered.'

'My stepfather's giving a party,' Claire said, 'for my brother's eighteenth birthday. I was told to invite any friends I like, but I haven't many. Will you come?'

'Love to. Thank you.'

Claire smiled at her and said impulsively, 'I'm so pleased that we met again, Jess.'

'Are you?' Jess looked down at her plate, her mouth wry. 'I wondered . . . If you hadn't rung me, I wouldn't have contacted you. It occurred to me that I'd rather thrust myself on you, the other night. Your . . . friend thought so, anyway.'

'Gareth? Oh, I'm sure he didn't!'

Jess shrugged, looking decidedly skeptical.

'Anyway,' Claire said, 'I did phone you, and I'm glad.'

Perhaps Jess had sensed that Claire didn't want to talk about Scott. At any rate, to Claire's relief, his name wasn't mentioned. As Claire made her way home she wondered how much Jess had guessed about her relationship with Scott . . . or how much he had told her. They had, after all, been friends for a long time. It was possible that Jess knew all about it. Shame made her face hot. Would he have told anyone? She didn't want to believe that he might even have boasted of his conquest . . . but it was possible.

Jess hadn't treated her any differently . . . but then, Jess wasn't the judging sort. Uneasily, Claire wondered where her friendship with Jess might lead, but remembering the odd, uncharacteristic diffidence of the other woman when she had said that she wouldn't have been the one to get in touch, she pushed her doubts aside. She still liked Jess very much. The disturbing memories evoked by her having been on the island at the same time as Scott would fade with time and be overlaid with fresh ones of Jess herself. Friendship was a rewarding thing, one of God's gifts to humanity, Mother Josephine would have said. Claire didn't want to turn her back on it.

Chapter Nine

Claire dressed carefully for the party. She wanted to do credit to her new family, and had allowed her stepfather to foot the bill for a new dress, while privately promising herself that it was the last time, and that the day after Jonnie's birthday she would definitely tackle Pietro and tell him that she intended to work for a living and could not possibly live forever on his charity.

The dress had been expensive, a filmy pale peach chiffon creation that left her arms and throat bare, clung to her slight figure as far as the waist, and then whirled into a romantic floating skirt. She wore silver sandals and a silver filigree bracelet, and left her hair loose to brush her shoulders. The pleased admiration with which Pietro greeted her appearance in the large lounge where they would entertain their guests, and the teasing whistles of her half-brothers, boosted her confidence further and convinced her that she had been right in this instance to accept her stepfather's generosity.

As the rooms gradually filled with people—mostly young friends of the boys', but with a sprinkling of older people who had known Jonnie from childhood —Claire began to look for the arrival of Jess. When she did come, she was late, and Claire noticed that she looked flushed and somewhat put out as she stood in the doorway looking about. Claire was moving towards her when Jess stepped into the room and allowed the man behind her to enter.

Automatically Claire's eyes travelled past her friend to the tall figure at her back. Her breath caught suddenly, and the room began to swirl about her slowly, before it settled into focus and she looked straight into Scott Carver's searching gaze.

She stopped dead and watched, as if in a dream, as Scott put a hand on Jess's arm and began steering her in Claire's direction.

Claire was still standing there stunned when her stepfather's voice rang out from somewhere behind her, above the babble of voices in the room. 'Scott! What a surprise—I didn't know you were back in Sydney!'

Bewildered, she watched Pietro step past her and clasp Scott by the upper arms, a broad smile on his often austere face. Scott seemed to watch her for a moment or two longer before he tore his gaze away from her stricken face and stepped back to shake Pietro's hand and return his greeting.

'And this . . . ?' Pietro turned his attention to Jess, his eyes overtly admiring in a very Italian way.

'This is Jess,' Scott explained blandly. 'The invitation was for her, but I told her you wouldn't mind me gate-crashing.'

'Mind? Of course not! My son, however . . .' Pietro grimaced comically. 'He invites a lovely lady to his birthday party, and she turns up with you . . . I can't answer for Giovanni, my friend!'

'Not your son, Pietro. Your . . . daughter, I believe, issued the invitation.'

'Claire? Oh, yes! She mentioned asking a friend—I thought . . . well, never mind.' He turned just as Claire was about to move away, blindly looking for a place to hide and pull herself together.

'Claire!' He beckoned imperiously, and she had no choice but to join him, standing beside him with a smile pinned to her face that she hoped reflected mild pleasure and not the chaotic emotions that were beginning to churn inside her.

Pietro put his arm about her shoulders. 'Your friend Jess is here, and this is Scott Carver, a friend of mine, but I haven't seen much of him lately. He's become a crusader.'

'Rot!' Scott intervened swiftly. 'Hello, Claire. How are you?'

She couldn't meet his eyes as she muttered, her voice husky with suppressed emotion, 'Fine, thank you. And you?'

He didn't answer for a moment, and she raised her eyes briefly to his, to see a queer blaze in the blue depths that sent her heart plunging erratically and shortened her breath. He shrugged and said, 'Let's discuss it later, shall we?'

Pietro looked quizzically from him to Claire and said, 'You know each other?'

'Slightly,' Claire said, carefully ignoring the lift of Scott's eyebrows. 'We met . . . a long time ago.'

'Well . . .' Pietro was puzzled, she could see, though he still smiled. 'Look after these two, Claire. I see that some more people are arriving.'

After he left them there was a fraught little silence. Then Jess said jerkily, 'I tried to tell Scott he couldn't come, but he wouldn't listen. He and your stepfather are old friends, apparently.'

Claire looked at her and saw the apology in her eyes. Wordlessly she touched Jess's arm, conveying her understanding. If Scott had made up his mind to accompany her, nothing Jess could have done would have stopped him. Evidently they had had a row about it, judging by the angry flush and bright eyes that made Jess look more attractive than ever, and the tautness that underlay Scott's urbane party manners.

'I'll get you both a drink,' she offered in stilted tones. 'What will you have?'

'I'll come with you,' Scott said. 'Wait for us, Jess.' He found a chair and almost pushed Jess into it, then placed his hand lightly on Claire's waist to guide her through the throng about the bar that had been set up in a corner of the room. 'Don't blame Jess,' he said in her ear. 'I saw the invitation you sent her, and insisted on coming.'

Bitterly she wished that she hadn't bothered to follow up her casual invitation over lunch with one of the formal embossed cards that Pietro had had printed for the party. She didn't know how much the other woman had guessed, or been told by Scott, about Claire, but she was fairly certain that Jess wouldn't have deliberately done this to her.

She shrugged and said with what she hoped was a convincing coolness, 'Pietro was pleased to see you. I expect he'd have sent you an invitation if he had known you were in Sydney.'

'He might have. Would you?'

They had reached the bar, and she said swiftly, 'I didn't even know you knew him. What would you like to drink?'

He asked for vodka, and another for Jess, which he let Claire carry while he took her gin and lime. She wondered if he had done it that way to make sure she couldn't slip away. She might have been able to do so otherwise, for as they turned with the drinks in hand, she was waylaid by some of Jonnie's friends, who tried to persuade her to join in the disco dancing in one of the other rooms, where the younger crowd was congregating. 'Maybe later,' she half-promised, laughing at them as they lamented the dearth of girls. 'I have a friend who's just arrived and is waiting for a drink.'

'Female?' they chorused eagerly.

'Yes, and I'll bring her too, if she'll come—after she's had a drink!'

Scott was looking at her oddly as the young men went off clutching cans of beer, and her smile faded under his penetrating eyes.

When they returned to Jess, they found her talking to Gareth, who had somehow found a seat alongside hers. He rose as they approached and gave up his chair to Claire. She introduced the two men and watched them appraise each other as they shook hands. They made an interesting contrast, Scott tall and tanned and broad-shouldered, and Gareth, almost as tall though leaner, but lithe and far from weedy, his features compared to Scott's more rugged good looks taking on an almost aristocratic cast.

Turning to Jess, she said, 'Sorry. I didn't mean to leave you alone like that. I'm glad Gareth found you.'

'Don't worry. Mr. Seymour has done his duty by me handsomely. He'd even have rushed off to the bar to get me a drink if I hadn't assured him that there was one on the way.' Jess looked up at Gareth and added, 'Thanks for the rescue act, but it wasn't really necessary. Do please go and talk to . . .'—she waved vaguely—'anyone you want.'

Gareth looked down at her with a decided gleam in his eye, but his voice was mild as he said, 'I'm fine here, thanks. If I stick around long enough for you to get a good look at me, you might even recognise me next time we meet.'

The flush had faded from Jess's cheeks, but now the colour rose again. 'I told you,' she said. 'I was thinking of something else.'

Gareth inclined his head slightly, ironically, and lifted the glass in his hand to finish his drink.

Jess was staring straight ahead, her lips compressed, and Claire sat toying with her drink, terribly conscious of Scott standing inches away, aware that he was watching her as he absently swirled the liquid in his glass. The noise of the party rose and fell about them, and for a few moments everything seemed to blur. Hoping that she was not going to faint, Claire took a gulp of her drink, and then another, and to her relief things seemed to swim back into perspective. She finished the gin in a third quick swallow and said brightly to Jess, 'Some of Jonnie's friends are short of dancing partners. I promised I'd try to persuade you to join them for a while. Want to come?'

'Sure,' Jess said. 'Why not?' She put down her half-finished vodka and rose. 'Where to?'

The young men welcomed them with open arms, and for half an hour they took part in the lively dancing, whirling from one partner to another. Then, as Claire turned laughingly away from a bronzed young giant who had been performing some extraordinary gyrations for her benefit, she found herself looking up into Scott's face and moving into his arms.

He held her closely, swaying to the rhythm of the music for a few minutes, then let her move away as the tempo quickened, dancing with masculine grace a few feet from her while he watched the supple motions of her body, before pulling her to him again, his hands firmly on her waist, his thighs touching hers.

'Where can we talk?' he asked quietly, his breath brushing her ear.

'It's a party,' she said, trying to sound lightly uncaring. 'And I'm hostessing, in a way. I'm afraid—'

'Don't start making excuses,' he cut in. 'I've got to talk to you, Claire.'

She tried to shift out of his embrace, but he only tightened his hold and stopped all pretence of dancing, standing still while other people wove about them.

Gritting her teeth and averting her eyes from him, she said, 'Let me go. I don't want to talk to you. I have nothing to say to you.'

He drew in an angry breath. 'We have a lot to say to each other, and you know it. For a start, what made you change your mind about entering the convent?'

She jerked her head back to stare at him accusingly. 'You should know that!'

His face reflected shock, and then a flash of something that might have been triumph, before it became peculiarly expressionless. 'You've got to see me, Claire . . . talk to me. If not tonight, how about tomorrow?'

'Not tonight, tomorrow, or ever. I've just told you, I have nothing to say to you! I don't want to see you again.'

His mouth hardened. 'Well, you're going to! I won't let you go so easily this time, Claire.'

'Is that a threat?' Her eyes sparkled with anger, clashing with the hard glitter of determination in his.

'I'm not threatening you,' he said softly. 'I'm telling you how it is, that's all. You can't go on running away forever. And when you stop, I'll be there. I promise.'

His face had changed, his eyes no longer angry but intent. But his mouth was a determined, stubborn line, and she was suddenly frightened.

'I don't want you!' she breathed. 'I don't want you in my life! Please . . .'

'Shh,' he said. 'Don't.' His hands became gentle, although he still held her. He moved them on her back, soothingly. 'You're panicking, and there's no need.' He grinned suddenly. 'What could I do to you, with all these people . . . ? Come on, let's dance.'

He began moving again to the music, and after a moment she followed blindly as his grip relaxed into a more conventional hold.

'You're gorgeous,' he murmured, looking at her dress and her shining hair. 'I always knew you could be.' He stroked a hand up her arm and touched her hair. His eyes held hers deliberately, letting her see his admiration. She shook her head in a slight negative movement, and his fingers caught at her hair, keeping her still for a second while he planted a brief hard kiss on her mouth.

She gasped, and stiffened in his arms.

'Relax.' He gave her a tiny shake. 'I won't do it again.'

'I don't want to dance anymore,' she said. 'I'm going back to the other room.'

He released her then, and she muttered something about finding her stepfather, and fled from him.

She managed to avoid being close to him for the rest of the evening. But it was a very long party, and when she finally fell into bed after all the guests had left, she was exhausted. She tried to think about other things—about Jonnie clowning with his friends, hugely enjoying himself; about Pietro proudly introducing her as his daughter to the guests who had not met her; about Gareth dancing with her, complimenting her on her dress and kissing her mouth lightly as he said good night.

But that brought back another memory—of Jess and Scott standing by the door together, watching, Jess with her mouth curled in one of her ironic little smiles, and Scott looking narrow-eyed and rather dangerous.

She wasn't really surprised when Scott came by

the flat the next afternoon. She wasn't quite prepared, however, for the adroit way he got her out of it. Thinking herself safe in the bosom of her new family, she had counted on their protection. But Scott saw Pietro first, and her stepfather was so sure she would enjoy a drive up the coast and a quiet dinner with his friend that he gave her no chance to refuse without being positively rude and having to explain her reasons to him.

She quietly seethed while Scott negotiated the road out of the city and onto the Pacific Highway, that passed through magnificent stands of spicy-scented eucalypts with an undergrowth of ferns before crossing the Hawkesbury River not far from where it joined the sea. Resolutely she stared at the changing scenery, the dark bush, the several green islands glimpsed from the bridge, the small settlements tucked into the bays that indented the shoreline. Eventually Scott left the Highway for a side road that twisted between sparser growth showing glimpses of the sea, and began to slacken his speed.

'You look very nice,' he commented at last, his gaze lingering on her bare shoulders. Her cool cream silk dress was held up by shoestring straps and belted with a narrow gold leather band that matched her gold sandals.

'Thank you,' she answered in a chilly voice, still gazing out the window at the passing gum trees and ferns.

'You're angry with me,' he said.

It was a frontal attack, and she turned toward him, meeting the hard questioning look in his eyes before he returned his concentration to the curving road ahead. 'Are you surprised?' she asked him waspishly. 'You know very well that I didn't want to go out with you. You got round my stepfather and made it impossible for me to refuse.'

'Not impossible.'

'Difficult, then!' she snapped.

'Okay, so I did. You could still have refused, though, if you'd really wanted to.'

'Not without giving reasons.'

Without looking at her, he said evenly, 'So you've told Pietro nothing about us?'

'There's nothing to tell.'

'I wouldn't say that.'

'I want to forget it,' she said in a low voice. 'Please, why won't you let me forget it ever happened?'

'Is that what you really want?'

'Yes!'

He glanced at her, his foot imperceptibly going down on the accelerator so that the car raced forward, gliding quickly through the trees and coming into sudden sunlight above a wide stretch of white sand, where the blue water broke into creamy foam as it met the beach.

He slowed then, and steered the car off the road, down to a spot near the sand where tall gums shaded them as he drew up near the trees.

Then he turned to her, his arm sliding along the back of the seat behind her, and looked fully at her. 'Can you forget it?' he demanded.

She turned away, staring blindly into the shadow of the trees, but he caught her chin and forced her to look at him. 'Can you?' he repeated.

Unexpectedly, tears welled in her eyes, spilling with shocking suddenness down her cheeks and running onto his fingers. He gave a harsh exclamation and released his grip to gather her into his arms. His mouth touched her wet cheeks and ruthlessly took her lips in a kind of angry desperation, his hands moving over her body and back again to her face to hold it between his palms as he kissed her, his thumbs wiping away the tears while he tried to draw a response from her.

Almost, she gave it. The remembered strength of his arms, the warm eroticism of his mouth against hers, the rise and fall of his hard chest against her breasts, were achingly familiar, calling up mind pictures of a tropical beach and a moonlit night and limbs entwined with each other in a fierce and gentle coming together.

Then the pressure of his mouth eased a little, and he murmured against her lips, 'You cried then, too. I remember. Why do you always cry?'

And she remembered the guilty remorse, the black despair, and with a sudden access of strength pushed herself away from him.

She huddled against the door, her shoulders hunched, her head in her hands, hiding her flushed and tear-wet face from him. She felt his hand on her arm and flinched, shuddering. 'Don't!' she said raggedly. 'Don't touch me. Leave me alone!'

His short, sharp sigh sounded exasperated. 'I didn't actually mean to,' he said. 'Until you cried. I was intending just to talk.'

'I told you before, we have nothing to talk about.'

'I don't accept that!'

She lifted her head then. 'Why? Why must you go on hounding me this way?'

'I'm not hounding you . . . I've simply invited you out for a drive and dinner.'

'Forced me, you mean!'

'I haven't used force . . . yet.'

She stared at him. 'That means you would!'

Angrily he said, 'All right, maybe I would . . . if I can't get you to see sense any other way.'

'You mean, if you can't get your way without resorting to violence.'

'I never used violence on you, Claire!' he said furiously. 'I didn't force you!'

'No.' She shook her head. 'No, I know you didn't. . . . It wasn't like that.'

She looked down at her hands twisting in her lap and willed them to be still. After a moment he said, above her bent head, 'Tell me what it was like for you, Claire.'

She threw him a look of horror and seemed to shrink back in her seat.

He bent closer, his voice soft. 'Stop pretending it didn't happen, darling. It happened, and we both loved it . . . you loved it. I know you did. I remember you lying under me on the sand, moving against me, the feel of you, your hands holding me. . . .'

'Stop! Stop it!' She covered her ears with her hands in torment. 'Why are you doing this to me? Haven't you done enough damage?'

'Damage?' He frowned, reaching for her hands, pulling them down. 'I didn't hurt you . . . I didn't! Not really. You said so at the time, and it was true. It was only moments before you were clinging to me again, asking me to go on. . . .'

She shook her head, her cheeks aflame, trying to twist away from him. 'That isn't what I meant,' she whispered. 'Don't you realise . . . ?' Her voice rose. 'You ruined everything! You took what you wanted, and it wrecked my life . . . everything I'd dreamed of, planned for . . . it was all . . . spoiled. For a few moments of pleasure. I can't forgive you for that . . . ever. That's why I couldn't go through with taking my vows. And I hate you for that. God forgive me, but I do. I think I'll hate you forever.'

She saw the shock hit him as she stared into his face. He said, 'Hate?' and his pupils dilated and then narrowed suddenly. Hoarsely he said, 'You can't hate me. I won't let you.'

Something inside her seemed to break through the bonds she had kept on it. Something hot and fierce rose and spread through her being, taking her over, claiming her body for its own. She laughed, a hard, mocking sound, quite unlike her usual quiet, low laughter. Her lips curled into a contemptuous smile. 'Try and stop me!' she said.

He went on staring at her as though she had suddenly turned into a stranger. As she had, she thought, slightly stunned. She didn't feel like herself, the girl who had wanted to be a nun, who had prayed for the grace to forgive this man who had sinned against her and against her God. That girl seemed to be standing aside, watching with astonishment the vengeful woman who had taken her place, who was filled with white-hot rage and exulting in it, her nails biting into her palms simply to stop herself from hitting out at the grim-faced man who sat beside her.

His expression changed, becoming no less grim, but more determined. His mouth thinned and his eyes narrowed, and as though he had come to a decision, he said softly, 'Okay. I will.'

Her eyebrows rose faintly, but she said nothing as he started the car again and drove up the slope to the road. She half-expected him to turn back and take her home, but he didn't. He drove for miles in silence, and then at last stopped again when it was nearly dusk, at a small cove with the breakers rolling in onto a strip of sand and spraying over the black rocks that jutted into the sea.

'Want to walk?' he asked her brusquely, not waiting for her nod before he got out and opened her door. She went ahead of him onto the sand, getting her sandals full of it in seconds, but not caring. They sat on the rocks, safe from the waves but close enough to feel the spray on their faces, and gradually Claire felt a kind of peace steal into her soul. They stayed until it was dark and the waves were white ghosts looming out of the star-laden sky and the tide had receded so that they no longer felt the damp kiss of foam on their skin with the boom and hiss of each breaker.

'Come on,' Scott said. Her sandals slipped on the wet rock as she stood up, and he shot out his hand and caught her, hauling her against him. She felt his shirt against her cheek, his arms about her back, and went rigid. For a moment he stood there holding her, and then he let her go and gripped her arm hard until they had regained the sand.

They walked in silence back to the car. He started back the way they had come and, after driving for some time, pulled in at a wayside restaurant, saying, 'Let's eat.'

She wasn't hungry, but it would have been childish to say so. She got out when he opened her door and went with him into the building.

They were taken to a table, and she said, 'You order. I'll be back shortly,' and left him to find her way to the ladies' room at the back of the restaurant.

As she combed her hair she looked in the mirror and regarded her reflection curiously. She felt that she ought to look different, but she didn't. Absently she touched up her mouth with pink lip gloss and used a smudge of shadow on her eyelids. Light makeup had already become a habit with her, and her months in the convent seemed a distant memory. But it was a memory that hurt, and although she no longer felt the white-hot fury that had consumed her so suddenly that afternoon, there was a core of hard anger within her that refused to go away. She came out and saw Scott sitting at the table with a drink in front of him, and stood looking at him coldly, thinking that but for him she would be safe now, cloistered behind the symbolic walls of the convent, unknowing and content. . . .

He looked up as she approached, watching her with unsmiling eyes, and indicated that he had got her a drink. She sat down and lifted the glass to her lips, sipping slowly. It was gin and lime, and the tart cool taste suited her mood.

'I ordered shellfish,' he said. 'I hope that's okay.'

'Fine.'

'I didn't know,' he said, staring at his drink, 'how you felt. . . .'

'I like seafood,' she said quickly.

He stared for a moment, because of course he hadn't been talking about her taste in food. Then he shrugged, his mouth twisting wryly, and said, 'I guess this isn't the time or place.'

There was no time or place for them, she wanted

to tell him. There never would be a time or a place again. All that was between them was in the past.

The tension was building unbearably, and to break it, she said, gazing round unseeingly at white-washed stone walls decorated with fishing nets and huge glass balls, 'This is nice.'

His breath escaped in a short, harsh laugh. 'Yes,' he said, his voice silkily smooth. 'Charming.'

Claire looked down, biting her lip. 'Have you been here before?'

'Once or twice.'

What a stilted conversation. She fought a curious desire to laugh hysterically. He had probably been here with other girls . . . women. It was that sort of place—dimly lit, the tables small and intimate, half-hidden from one another by alcoves and greenery, and on the terrace outside, overlooking the sea, a few couples were sitting with their drinks in a dim glow cast by imitation antique carriage lamps fastened to the walls.

She supposed that those couples would end their evening with a romantic interlude, as Scott had probably done before, when he had brought other women here. Disturbed at the trend of her thoughts, she was glad when the waiter placed their meals in front of them. She tried to concentrate on the food and found, surprisingly, that she was hungry after all.

She refused a sweet course, though, and Scott too went straight on to coffee.

'Here or on the terrace, sir?' the waiter asked, and without looking at Claire, Scott said instantly, 'Here.' Apparently, like her, he couldn't wait for the day to be over so that he could take her home.

He drove the rest of the way back to Sydney very fast, confirming her impression, and when she risked a glance at him he was frowning, his hands gripping the wheel very hard. She thought he might let her get out of the car on her own, and drive away and out of her life for good, but although she opened the door as soon as he drew to a halt outside the flats, he was beside her as she made her way up the steps into the lobby.

She turned to face him then. 'I'll be all right now,' she said, politely dismissing. 'Thank you for the drive and the dinner.'

She could feel a tautness in him and didn't quite meet his eyes, afraid of what she might see there. But he didn't move, and after a second or two she turned away—only to be jerked back by a forceful hand on her wrist, spinning her round and into his arms.

Automatically her head went back in alarm, and she caught a glimpse of blazing blue eyes before his mouth found hers, devastatingly, his lips hard and searching and inescapable.

She couldn't fight him, but neither would she give in, even when the kiss became more gentle, his mouth moving persuasively against hers, rousing memories that she didn't want to recall.

He stopped kissing her, but his arms still held her, and he looked down into her wide-open eyes and said, 'You said to try and stop you hating me.'

Claire swallowed and ran her tongue over her throbbing mouth. 'That isn't the way.'

A faint, derisive smile touched his mouth. 'Isn't it? It's the best way I know.'

'It's the only way you know. Take what you want and run.'

Anger blazed in his eyes. 'I didn't run! You did. You wouldn't wait for me. I asked you to wait.'

'Wait on your pleasure? No thanks. Why don't you admit that you were relieved to find me gone when you came back to the island?'

'Relieved?' he said explosively, his hold on her loosening so that she was able to break free. 'What gave you that idea?'

'Weren't you?' she challenged him.

'No, I was not! If you want to know, I was bloody angry at first. I'm still angry. How could you, Claire? How could you just walk away without a word?'

It hadn't been easy. But she wouldn't tell him that. 'Aren't you used to it?' she taunted. 'Or were you angry because usually you're the one who does the walking out, when *you're* tired of an affair?'

He looked at her in taut silence for several seconds. Then he said slowly, 'I see. You've always seen me as some sort of Don Juan, haven't you? Does it make you feel better to think you were just another conquest, a notch in my belt?'

'Well, I was, wasn't I? You certainly couldn't claim to be as innocent as—'

'As you were, my bogus little nun?' he said cruelly. 'Okay, so I was thirty years old and not a monk. Not pure and unsullied, like you. But I don't recall you asking for details of my past experience on the beach that night. When you came walking towards me, out of the water, you knew me . . . you knew what was going to happen. And you wanted it as badly as I did. I don't care what your puritan conscience says about it now, or how you've managed to dirty it in your narrow little mind since; I'm not sorry it happened, and you can't make me feel guilty about it. It was beautiful and good, and nothing will make me believe that it was wrong! And one day you'll admit that, too.'

Claire was shaking her head, denying everything he said. There was a great gulf between them that could never be bridged, a gulf of anger and accusation and differing beliefs that would always keep them apart, and just for a moment her anger seemed to split apart and reveal the grief and despair that underlay it. But that hurt too much, and determinedly she held on to her anger, facing him with it, not allowing it to disintegrate into tears. 'No,' she said. 'You'll never make me do that.'

This time, when she turned away from him towards the stairs, he didn't try to stop her. But she knew now that he was not going to leave her alone, that the battle had only just begun.

Chapter Ten

 $\mathscr{I}$ t seemed, though, that he was preparing to play a waiting game. He became a frequent visitor, encouraged by Pietro and popular with Jonnie and Paul, who accepted invitations to sail with him that Claire turned down. He would go off with them, apparently quite content to have their company instead of hers, but he always came back to the house, and without being so pointed about it that questions would be asked, she found it impossible to avoid him altogether.

Pietro teased him about his 'crusade,' and although Scott refused to be drawn on the subject, she gathered that he had in some way 'adopted' the mission station on the island, and now visited it on a fairly regular basis. He had supplied prefab emergency housing with funds from his own company and had persuaded others, such as Pietro's, to donate similar aid to other islands after the hurricane. He was also helping the islanders to organise an agricultural program that would bring their food supplies back to subsistence level in the shortest possible time, so that they need no longer rely on outside assistance.

Unable to stop herself, she asked him one day for news of the sisters and Jacob the gardener and some of her erstwhile pupils, and didn't even notice when the two boys went off to play their latest tape in their own room and Pietro quietly got up and went out, leaving her alone with Scott.

'Thomas?' he was saying, trying to match a face to the name she had given him.

'A tall, thin boy,' she said. 'He's extremely intelligent . . . about twelve?'

'Oh, yes! He helps around the hospital sometimes.'

'Does he? Oh, good. He told me he'd like to be a doctor someday. I didn't like to be too encouraging, because I don't know how he could afford the education, and he'd have to travel a long way from home for his training. . . .'

'I'll help,' Scott said quietly. 'When he's old enough, and if he still feels the same way.'

'Oh, would you? He's a serious soul; I don't think he'll change his mind.' She paused, then said slowly, 'You've done a lot for them, haven't you . . . the islanders?'

'No,' he said shortly. 'I've done a little to help, that's all. A drop in the bucket.'

'You once told me you weren't . . . any sort of philanthropist. Or words to that effect.'

He shrugged. 'I said I felt helpless. The problems of poverty, illiteracy, disease . . . they've always seemed so vast, so unsolvable. You fix the problems in one place, but they crop up somewhere else, just as desperately. Sometimes solving one actually creates another that's ten times worse. Maybe I couldn't see the wood for the trees. The island . . . it's different, somehow. I can see the immediate needs, and I know the people. I never before felt that poverty and all that goes with it were my problem. But these people *are* my problem. . . . I care about them. So you see, I'm still no philanthropist. I can't see the abstract problem in perspective, only the one that's right under my nose. Although I admit that seeing what we've been able to do in one small place has made me more interested in trying the same methods elsewhere. I'm chairman of a hurricane-relief committee, did you know?' He grinned self-deprecatingly, as though she should find that funny in light of what she knew of him. 'We can see the end of the short-term relief actions now, but we may rename the committee and carry on with long-term projects designed to make future disasters less devastating.'

She watched him as he spoke, his face intent and serious. It was true, she realised. He cared about helping; it was important to him.

'What happened to your need for challenge?' she asked quietly.

He looked surprised, then laughed. 'I get all the challenge I need out of this at the moment. And out of . . . you.'

He had suddenly brought them back to a personal level, and she got to her feet, intent on fleeing.

He got up too, blocking her way to the door. 'Don't run away,' he said. 'You do it too often.'

'It's no use, Scott,' she said. 'Find somebody else.'

'I don't want somebody else. I want you.'

'No,' she said. 'Never again.'

'I want you,' he repeated. 'I wanted you from the first time I saw you, when I thought you were a nun and unattainable. . . .'

'That's why,' she said. 'The attraction of the unattainable, the challenge to your . . . masculinity. You never saw me, just a woman in a veil. And you wanted to pull aside the veil. Well, you did it . . . once.'

'Once wasn't enough, Claire.'

'It was more than enough for me.'

He looked at her, his eyes narrowed and glittering. 'Was it?' he asked softly. 'Are you sure about that, my darling?'

When he came towards her, she stood still, since he wasn't going to let her run away, and gathered her forces. She felt his hands slide gently up her arms, moulding her shoulders, lingering on her throat and then cupping her head between them. She kept her face calm and looked back at him with quiet defiance, bringing a slight spark of anger to his eyes. He lowered his mouth with infinite slowness, tilting her head to just the angle he wanted, and she heard him whisper, 'How sure are you, little nun?'

She closed her mouth tightly against him, trying to ignore the tantalising soft kisses he pressed on it, the insistent nibbling on her lower lip, then the upper one, the intrusiveness of his tongue at the corner of her mouth. She felt heat washing over her, tiny ripples of excitement starting in her stomach in spite

of her determination not to give in, and she made a
stifled sound of despairing protest and wrenched her
mouth away.

His eyes were glittery, and he didn't let her go far.
His hands tightened on her cheeks, and his thumbs
probed, pressing at the angle of her jaw so that she
was forced to open her mouth, and then he kissed
her again, not gently, but with a passion that made
her heart pound. She brought her hands up involuntarily to touch him, running her fingers along his
upper arms to his shoulders, pressing against him as
his own hands left her face to slide down her back
and bring her arching into the hard curve of his
body.

She shivered, although she was consumed with
heat, and felt the response she had aroused in him as
he pressed her even closer, his hands insistent,
wanton, beautiful. . . .

She surfaced, gasping, from the kiss, and heard
him say, with his lips in her hair, 'You haven't
forgotten . . . it was just like this, wasn't it?' He
moved his lips against her throat almost feverishly,
and in muffled tones said, 'You were fantastic . . .
unlike any other woman. . . .'

She cried out, '*No!*' and pushed against him,
feeling his hands fall away in shock, then grab for
her again as she fought him, hitting at his chest and
shoulders, sobbing, 'No, leave me alone . . . Scott
. . . *Don't!*'

'*Scott?*' It was Pietro's voice, loud and ominous,
and she realised that Scott had released her and had
turned to face her stepfather, who stood in the
doorway.

She took a deep, shuddering breath and looked up

to see Pietro closing the door quietly behind him, his expression austere in the extreme. 'You will please explain this, Scott,' he said, fixing a hard stare on the younger man. 'You know that I regard Claire as my daughter, and you as a friend whom I have trusted. Must I withdraw my trust?'

Claire said, 'It's all right, Papa. . . . I can handle it. . . .'

'No.' He made a silencing, imperious gesture with his hand. 'You are under my protection, Claire. I have noticed that you decline Scott's invitations. . . . I think perhaps you prefer Gareth Seymour. That's your business; they are both good men . . . or so I thought. I haven't wanted to interfere in your affairs, but I won't have you hurt or insulted, especially while you are living in my home. And I will have an answer from Scott.'

'You'll have it,' Scott said evenly.

But Claire interrupted. 'He kissed me, that's all. There's really no need for—'

'And did she not make it clear,' Pietro said to Scott with dry sarcasm, 'that she did not wish to be kissed by you?'

'Not exactly,' Scott drawled with equal dryness. 'Actually, she kissed me back . . . unmistakably.'

Pietro's eyebrows rose skeptically. He turned his keen eyes on Claire, who was standing silent and scarlet-cheeked. 'Claire?'

Dumbly she nodded. 'At first . . .' she managed to whisper.

Pietro's expression relaxed suddenly into a beautiful understanding. 'Ah . . . I perceive the problem,' he said, and looked reprovingly at Scott, then crossed to put his arm about Claire's shoulders. 'You have been clumsy, my friend; I'm surprised at you. I thought you would have more . . . finesse. Did you not understand that Claire is an innocent? She has not had the experience of lovemaking that most young women have today. You went too fast and frightened her, that's all. . . .'

'Papa . . . please!'

'Shh,' he said, placing an admonishing finger on her lips. 'Don't worry, my chicken. We'll sort this out. Scott . . .' He paused, then went on, 'I know it's old-fashioned to ask a man his intentions these days, but then, as I've explained, Claire is an old-fashioned girl . . . in some ways.' He smiled down teasingly, reassuringly, at her as she stood in the crook of his arm. 'I will not allow you to hurt her, so . . . you must tell me, if you please, if this interest of yours is serious . . . because if you are looking for only a light, temporary love affair, Claire is not for you.'

Scott looked him fully in the face and said, 'It's serious, all right. I want to marry her.'

Claire felt as if she had been hit in the stomach. She gasped, and her hand flew to her mouth, her teeth closing on her knuckle.

Pietro was smiling. 'Then I give you permission to court my daughter,' he said. 'But, of course, she must make her own decision. I have warned you already, you have a rival. And,' he added sternly, loosening his hold on Claire's shoulder, 'there will be no repetition of this . . . episode? I'm sure I can rely on that.'

Scott smiled faintly, measuring Pietro, his eyes wry. Then he nodded. 'Yes. You can.'

'Good. I will leave you two to make up.'

Claire tried to detain him, 'Papa . . .'

But he took her hand from his sleeve, holding it for a moment between his own. 'You have nothing to fear, Claire. I have known Scott for a long time, and I trust his word. Besides, I'll be close by. No one will force you to do anything.'

When he had gone she said, 'You didn't need to say that.'

'I know. But I meant it.'

'You *don't* want to marry me!'

'You don't even know what *you* want,' he said scathingly, 'so how the hell do you presume to know what *I* want?'

'I *do* know what I want! And it isn't you!'

'Isn't it? You wanted me just five minutes ago . . . desperately, I'd have said. And don't tell me I imagined it, because I *know* I'm right.'

'Oh, you'd know, all right! You've had so much experience, haven't you?'

He groaned. 'Do we have to go over that again? What about Gareth Seymour? Is he without "experience"?'

'No.' She coloured and then said, 'I don't know. I don't think so. He's very . . .'

'Very what?' he queried when she halted.

Very good at kissing, she was thinking. But it wouldn't do to say it aloud. She had no intention of allowing Scott an opening with a provocative remark like that. 'Nothing,' she said. 'It's none of your business, anyway.'

'He's interested in Jess,' Scott said brutally. He watched her, looking for a reaction.

'Jess?' she said cautiously. 'What makes you say that?'

He shrugged, looking rather satisfied. 'There are certain signs. He doesn't really mean a thing to you, does he?'

She realised that perhaps she should have pretended a consuming interest. 'I'm very fond of him.'

He grinned, making her long to hit him for his complacency. 'That's what Jess said when I accused her of trying to take your boyfriend. "She's fond of him." She also said she didn't like him herself.'

Fascinated in spite of herself, Claire asked, 'And does she?'

'She doesn't know it, but I think she's falling for him. And fighting it. I don't envy him.'

'Jess deserves to be happy.'

He was regarding her narrowly. After a moment he said, 'Don't you?'

She shrugged. 'That's an odd question.'

'Not so odd. When I came back to the island that first time and found you gone, I had a talk with Father Damien . . . a long one. That was after I got over wanting to go after you and break every bone in your body.'

She winced, and he said, 'Yes. That's how I felt—when I wasn't wanting to find you and make love to you until you stopped seeing, wanting, feeling anything but me. Don't look like that; I'm not going to touch you.'

She took a shaky breath and sat down on the nearest chair. He stood looking down at her for a while, then sat down too, facing her. 'I didn't tell him what had happened,' he said. 'But . . . well, I got a lot of answers to hypothetical questions. I gather that making love with me was a major sin, in your eyes. I know you feel guilty about it. I said before, I can't pretend I'm sorry that it happened. Don't you remember how right it all seemed? How *meant?* But . . . I'm sorry for the way you feel about it. Sorry that it's turned into a shameful memory for you, instead of a bright, shining one.'

She couldn't look at him, but he got up and came over to her, then squatted in front of her chair, putting his hands over hers in her lap. 'Claire . . . won't it make it right if you marry me?'

'No,' she said baldly. 'No. You can't give back what you've taken from me. It's very noble of you to try, but it's much too late to be noble. You could have tried some of this self-sacrifice on the beach that night.'

He stood up abruptly. 'So could you!'

She flinched away from him, and he said, 'Forget I said that. I didn't mean to throw it up at you. And I'm not being noble, either. You don't think I offered to marry you to make an honest woman of you, or because your father wants me to state my honourable intentions, do you?'

'Didn't you?'

'Oh, for God's sake! You're not stupid! You know damn well I want you so much it's tearing me apart. I've never stopped wanting you since that night on the island.'

'Me and how many others?'

'None.'

She looked up then, disbelievingly, to find him regarding her steadily, his mouth stubborn.

'None,' he repeated. 'No one. Only you.'

Claire swallowed. 'So badly?'

'Yes.'

She couldn't take it in. It put their whole relationship in a totally different perspective. She looked and looked at him, and saw that he was telling the truth.

He was the despoiler, the man who had taken her virginity, and with it her whole life as she had planned it, who had snatched away the comforting security of the convent and made her face the world naked and alone. And he was putting himself in her power.

Frightened, she stood up, her face pale as she said quickly, her voice high with strain, 'No . . . I can't marry you. I won't.'

His face took on a shuttered look, his mouth thinning. He said, 'No one's forcing you. But I won't give up, Claire. There's no one else for you . . . there never has been, and that gives me an edge.'

'You're quite ruthless, aren't you?'

'You always thought that of me. If I give you reason, can you blame me?' He laughed, not waiting for her to reply, and said, 'Yes, of course you will. You blame me for everything . . . all of it. It saves you from examining your own conscience, doesn't it?'

'That's not true!'

'No?' He looked at her steadily. 'Think about it.'

But she had already thought about it too much, and after he had gone, leaving her feeling wrung out, pale and listless, she switched on the television, ignoring Pietro's gleaming, curious glances, and tried to immerse herself in a cops-and-robbers drama. It didn't work, but she doggedly sat through both it and a late-night movie, hoping that she would then be tired enough to sleep in spite of the insistent thoughts spiralling in her brain.

When she did, it was to dream of a beach in the moonlight, and of gentle hands on her body, fingertips tracing its outline, making her tingle with warm desire, and she woke with Scott's name on her lips, heard it shockingly spoken into the quiet air of morning.

The echo of the dream lingered, her skin still alive with longing, and she moaned and turned her face into the pillow and fought against the bittersweet memories that had haunted her in the six months of her aborted postulancy and finally sent her back into the world, away from the life she had wanted so much.

'I can't marry him; I *can't!*' she whispered in anguish. Then, 'I mustn't.'

'I can't,' she repeated to Mother Josephine a few days later in the convent parlour.

'But you want to?' the nun suggested quietly.

'No! I . . . No.'

Mother Josephine clasped her hands before her, regarding Claire with interest and not a little sympathy. At last Claire had told her the whole story of her relationship with Scott Carver, grateful that the mother superior had listened patiently, without expressing disapproval, without commenting at all. 'But if you were sure, there would be no problem, would there?' she said now. 'What troubles you, child? Your love for him? Or your hatred?'

Claire opened her mouth in shock, then shook her head slightly. 'I . . . I . . . How did you know?'

'I know you well, and listening to you, watching your face . . .' Mother Josephine spread her hands. 'My dear, it's obvious. Of course you love him. You loved him enough to give yourself to him in spite of all your scruples and your upbringing. And you love him still, but your resentment of him is getting in the way.'

'I shouldn't have. . . .' Claire said unhappily. 'I know I shouldn't have. . . .'

'But you did,' Mother Josephine reminded her gently. 'And now you must cope with the consequences. Had you not been intimate, perhaps you might have got over it, taken a new direction . . . even remained here with us, though I doubt that. I don't think you were meant for the religious life, and it's true that God moves in mysterious ways . . . also that he can make good come of what the world calls evil. Claire . . . you're such a wholehearted person, in love, in hatred, in dedication to what you believe in, what you want. Once you gave yourself to this man, perhaps in some way you bound yourself to him forever. I think that's what you feel, deep down, isn't it?'

Claire stared straight ahead, thinking. 'Perhaps,' she acknowledged. 'But . . . surely *you* don't think I should marry him? He's not a Catholic, or even a Christian. . . . He's an unbeliever. He doesn't feel at all guilty about . . . what we did. He refuses to feel guilty. He resents it that I do.'

'Have you fallen in love with a charming hedonist?'

'No. No, he's more than that. He might have been, once, but not now. He cares about people.' For some reason his long friendship with Jess came to mind, and she recalled how he had been there when Jess had needed him. But she told Mother Josephine about his work for the islanders instead, and his plans for the future of the hurricane-relief committee.

'So,' the nun said, 'he's a good man, though not of our faith.'

'Isn't that important?'

'Of course it is. But not, perhaps, of overriding importance. When the partners love each other and practise tolerance, mixed marriages can sometimes be very successful. Would he resent your practising your faith, perhaps?'

'No, I'm sure he wouldn't.'

'And your children?'

'Mother—'

'Would he let the children learn about your religion, and not resent it?'

'I think so. He's not a bigoted man. But—'

'But that isn't really the point. I know. You pulled out that red herring for me, Claire.'

Claire bit her lip. 'I'm sorry. But it wasn't only for you.'

'Well, perhaps you've been manufacturing reasons for yourself, too. The real crux of the matter is something entirely different. You're afraid.'

'Yes.'

'Of what?'

'I think you know.'

'It may help if you put it into words.'

Claire stood up and walked to the window. The nun watched her, remembering that nearly two years ago Claire had done the same thing, trying to sort out her feelings for her mother. On that occasion Sister Josephine had joined her, touched her, put her arm around her. This time she sat still, waiting. Claire was no longer a girl, but a woman, making a woman's decision. Almost to herself, the nun said, 'I wish I could advise you what to do, my dear. I could say, refuse him, send him away, go away yourself. He seduced you and showed no remorse; he's an unbeliever, and in the old days that would have been enough to make any religious adviser say, "Give him up; forget him and marry someone of your own faith." Now the answers are less cut-and-dried. Who knows where God is leading you? Perhaps you could be the means of conversion for this man. Or, on the other hand, he may endanger your faith. I hope not. I think that you're strong enough to withstand the pressures.'

Without looking round, Claire said, 'I don't think I'm strong at all. I've shown how weak I am in the face of temptation. And now I feel so . . . mixed up. If he had kept out of my life, perhaps in time there might have been someone else for me. But not now. I don't know if he loves me, or if it's just . . . I don't know. He hasn't said he does.'

'Have *you?*'

Claire shook her head. 'I didn't even know . . . until you said so just now. I just felt . . . muddled, and furious. I thought . . . I thought it was all hate. Because he did spoil my life. I would have gone through with it, made my vows. . . . I'd have been a *good* nun! I know you don't think so, but . . .'

'I never said that. I said I didn't think you had a true vocation. You'd have been good . . . and un-happy.'

Claire shook her head, hardly listening. 'It was the white dress, the wedding dress,' she said. 'Every time I looked at it I knew I had no right to wear it, and . . . I couldn't.'

'And you blame Scott Carver for that. I wonder if that's quite fair. If you were taking a wrong path, God would surely have shown you that in some way.'

Claire turned, her eyes tormented. 'You've always been so sure it was wrong.'

'No, not sure. But uneasy about you. You would insist on running away from life, shutting yourself up in here with us because we made you feel safe.'

'Scott said I was always running away.'

'There comes a time when there's nowhere to run to.'

'Yes. I think I've reached it. I . . . I'm sorry . . . I can't tell you all of it . . . the feelings. I don't have the words.'

'Tell him.'

'*Him?* Scott?'

'Yes. Scott. It's between you and him, isn't it? He's asked you to marry him. You must be honest with him . . . whatever your answer is going to be.'

She had already answered him, of course, but he had told her that he wouldn't accept her refusal, panicking her into going to her old refuge, Mother Josephine and the convent. Since then he had, surprisingly, not been to the house, but she knew better than to think he had changed his mind. He had said he would be back, and he would.

It was from Jess, over lunch in one of the city's busy restaurants one day, that she learned that Scott had left Sydney on another visit to the island.

'I'm surprised he didn't tell you,' Jess said. 'I thought you two had been seeing each other a lot.'

'He's a friend of my stepfather's,' Claire said. 'He comes to the house quite often.'

'Oh,' Jess drawled, her shrewd eyes disbelieving. 'I figured things weren't going too well. Scott's been like a bear with a sore paw just lately. What are you doing to him, Claire?'

'Nothing.'

Jess shrugged. 'Okay, I'll mind my own business. Only . . . Oh, never mind.'

'Only what?'

'Just . . . you're not happy either, are you? I'm not sure what's going on, but if I can help at all . . . you know where to find me.'

'Thanks. I may just hold you to that. One thing you might do.'

'Yes?'

'Tell me when Scott gets back.'

'Sure thing.'

'Scott said you've been seeing Gareth.'

Jess looked down at her cigarette, and her lips pursed a little. 'He's wrong.'

'Oh? He said . . .' Claire faltered as Jess looked up, cold rejection in her eyes.

Jess said, 'He was probably trying to find out if you were jealous. You have no need to be. Gareth Seymour doesn't interest me in the least.'

'I'm not jealous. You told me yourself that I'm not in love with him.'

Jess looked at her consideringly. 'That doesn't mean he's not in love with you.'

'I'm sure he isn't. Jess . . . you haven't been holding back because of me, have you?'

'My dear girl, *you* may be the self-sacrificing type,

but I'd have thought you'd know by now that I'm not. I've just told you, the man is of no interest to me whatsoever.'

'Speak of the devil,' Claire said. 'He's just come in.'

Jess looked at her suspiciously. 'You didn't set this up, did you, Claire? Because if you did, I don't think I'll ever forgive you!'

'No, I swear I didn't. Anyway, he isn't alone.'

'Oh?' Jess swivelled to have a look at the smartly turned-out young woman by Gareth's side. 'Well,' she drawled, stubbing out her cigarette. 'He seems to be doing all right for himself, doesn't he?'

Claire watched in fascination as Jess's strong, elegant fingers ground the half-smoked cigarette to a pulp in the glass ashtray. Then Gareth was beside them with the woman, saying, 'Hello, Claire . . . Jess.'

Claire smiled uncertainly as Jess said with elaborate casualness, 'Oh, hello . . . Gareth.'

She saw a look pass between them that she couldn't fathom. Jess looked cool and distant, and Gareth faintly amused, but as their eyes clashed for a moment there seemed to be some sort of electrical charge in the air.

Then Gareth drew his companion forward and introduced her as Mrs. Faulkner. Jess acknowledged the introduction with perfect politeness, then said, 'What a pity we've just finished. You might have joined us.'

Gareth's mouth twitched, but he said smoothly, 'We have a table reserved, anyway. But it's kind of you to think of it.'

Claire was fairly sure that kindness was far from Jess's mind, and that Gareth was well aware of it. When he and the woman on his arm had gone to their corner table, she said, 'What was that all about?'

'What?' Jess asked innocently.

Claire gave up. Shaking her head, she smiled and said, 'All right, never mind.'

Getting a job was not quite as simple as Claire had expected. Teaching positions were few and far between at mid-term, and she wasn't at all sure that she really wanted to return to teaching in any case.

But she did manage to get a place serving behind the counter in a small specialty shop near King's Cross. They handled tourist wares and handicrafts from all over the world, and when she unpacked a crate of carved teak masks, traditional figures and birds from the Solomons, she experienced a pang of something almost like homesickness.

She thought of Scott, back there now, and pictured him talking to the missionaries and the natives, seeing his slanting smile as he conversed with Jacob or Thomas or Sister Amy, his fair head glinting in the sun. Scott and Jess had never condescended to the islanders, never put them down as the others in the party had tended to do. He was, as Sister Josephine had said, as Jess kept saying in different ways, a good man.

Neither of them saw any great barrier to her marrying him. The barrier was within herself, and she had to work it out for herself. No one, in the end, could advise her. It wasn't a decision to be made by other people.

Claire had hoped to have some warning of Scott's return, had made and discarded tentative plans for moving out of her stepfather's home, finding a place of her own and leaving instructions that he was not to be told where she was. But that was running away again, and she firmly took herself in hand and made up her mind to stay and face him, whatever it cost.

In the event, she had no chance to avoid him. She was visiting Jess, in her restored colonial cottage in the old suburb of Parramatta, when there was a rap on the door, and Jess went out into the narrow little hall to open it. Claire, sitting on the antique sofa with a cup of tea in her hand, heard her say, 'Scott! When did you get back?' And his deep voice said in reply, 'This morning. Pleased to see me?'

'As ever! How's the island? Come on in. I've got another visitor.'

'I don't want to intrude . . .' he was saying as they appeared in the doorway. He stopped there abruptly as Jess walked back into the room, her eyes apologetic as they met Claire's, but unable to hide her pleasure in Scott's return.

Claire put down her cup on the end table near the sofa and rose to her feet. 'I'll be going,' she said to Jess, and managed a small, uneasy smile at Scott. 'Nice to see you again, Scott.'

'You don't need to go yet,' Jess said, and Scott drawled, 'Hello, Claire.' To Jess he said, 'She's running away from me. She always does.'

'Why?' Jess demanded. 'What have you done to her?'

He laughed. 'You're turning into a mother hen, Jess. Actually, Claire can look after herself quite well.'

He was still standing in the doorway, and Jess said, 'Well, if you're coming in, sit down, for heaven's sake. You're too big for this place.'

'After you,' he said to Claire, moving only a little way into the room. 'If you're really in a hurry to go someplace, I'll drive you. Finish your tea.'

Defeated, she sat down again. She had to face him sometime, and it might as well be now, with Jess there to ease some of the tension between them.

It wasn't so very difficult, and Jess made every effort to keep the conversation general, getting him to talk about his latest visit to Afiuta. Father Damien was working like a beaver, helping the islanders to install pipes for clean water convenient to the villages; the new hospital water supply was working better than the old one ever had; there was a new school, and a native teacher trained in Rabaul was doing wonders with the children.

'I'd love to go back there,' Claire said involuntarily.

Scott looked at her coolly. 'Would you? Come with me sometime.'

She laughed and shook her head.

'Why not?' he pursued relentlessly. 'What are you doing with yourself, anyway? I can't see you living a life of leisure for long. Your conscience is too active.'

'I'm not living a life of leisure,' she told him somewhat sharply. 'I have a job.'

'Doing what?'

'Selling. It's in a shop.'

'With your qualifications?'

'I like it,' she said defiantly. 'It's a handicraft shop. We sell a lot of interesting stuff.' . . . Some of it comes from the islands.'

He looked interested. 'Any outlet for some handiwork produced by a village cooperative? We're trying to organise markets in Australia for the island work, sold direct instead of through middlemen, who rake off half the profit.'

'I don't know,' she said. 'I'd have to ask the proprietor.'

'Do,' he said decisively. 'Please.'

'Perhaps you should speak to her yourself. I'll tell her to expect to hear from you, if you like?'

'Good.' He smiled at her, and for one moment the hard lump of anger that settled in her chest every time she saw him dissolved, and she smiled back.

'I must go,' she said. 'My stepfather is expecting guests tonight, and I'm supposed to be there.'

He rose too, insisting on driving her, and Jess shrugged and grimaced at Claire behind his back, indicating that she might as well accept gracefully.

Chapter Eleven

In the car he said, 'Did you miss me, Claire?'

'No.' She was staring straight ahead at the windscreen.

'Liar.'

'Egotist.'

He laughed. 'You pack quite a punch beneath that meek exterior, don't you? When are you going to marry me?'

'I turned you down, remember?'

'I remember. I hoped you'd have changed your mind by now. It seemed to me, just now at Jess's place, that maybe you weren't hating me quite so much.'

'That's hardly a basis for marriage.'

'I'm going to do it, you know. Stop you hating me. Make you love me.'

'You can't force a thing like that!' she protested.

'I know. I'm not talking about force. Forget what I said about that. I was wild with fury and frustration at the time. You needn't be afraid of me, Claire.'

'I'm not afraid of you.'

He glanced at her frowningly. 'You're afraid of something. I feel it every time I come near you.'

Was it so obvious? Mother Josephine had sensed it, too. What would they both say, she wondered, if she told them she was afraid of herself?

He suddenly put his hand over hers, where they were clasped together in her lap. 'Don't worry,' he said quietly. 'We'll work it out in the end. Whatever it is that bothers you, I wish you'd tell me.'

He waited, but she said nothing. His touch had wakened echoes, memories, and she was fighting warring desires to hold his hand to her cheek and to throw it off in violent rejection. Every time he laid a finger on her it caused the same confusing wave of emotion. She wanted him to go further, hold her, kiss her, and make love to her, but along with that violent need was another, equally violent reaction, a burning, barely controllable anger that he could make her feel like that so easily, that he had made her feel it that night on the island and taken advantage of it to make her throw away all her upbringing, go against her most basic beliefs, discard in a moment of blind passion a whole lifetime of peace and happiness.

After a while he sighed and removed his hand. 'You're going away from me again, aren't you?' he said. 'But I'm coming after you, Claire. And I'll keep on coming until you stop and wait for me.' He paused. 'Have you seen Gareth while I was away?'

'Once.'

He looked at her sideways, and she saw his knuckles tighten on the wheel. Something made her add, 'I was lunching with Jess. He came in with a woman. A Mrs. Faulkner.'

'Désirée Faulkner?'

'I don't know. She was blond and very . . . expensive-looking.'

He smiled faintly. 'That's Désirée. Well, well.' He frowned abstractedly, and she said, 'Why do you say it like that?'

'I'd heard she was in the process of getting a divorce. Is Gareth acting for her?'

'I've no idea. He didn't say.'

'How did Jess take it?'

'Jess says she has no interest in Gareth.'

'I know what she *says.*'

'Well . . .'

'If he hurts her, I'll break him.'

'I think you're in love with Jess yourself.'

'Jealous, darling? Jess is a good friend. I'm not in love with her. It's you I want, and you know it.'

Stubbornly she shook her head. She wasn't jealous. She had a feeling that he was right about Jess. Her lack of interest in Gareth was a pretence. She hoped they would work it out, and remembering Gareth's attitude to Jess, thought that there was some hope. Probably he *was* acting for the Faulkner woman, and the lunch had been a business one. She might hint as much to Jess. But she couldn't run her friends' lives for them. There were enough complications in her own.

When Scott stopped the car outside her home he

took her hand in his before she could open the door, and held it firmly, saying, 'Jess kissed me hello. How about you?'

'I'm sure Jess did a good job,' she said.

'One kiss. Will it hurt you?'

Yes, she thought. Yes, unbearably. But he was coming closer, very gently putting his hand to her cheek, turning her to face him. 'I'll take it slowly this time,' he said. 'I know I made a mistake before, pushed you into something you didn't really mean to happen. It's going to be different now, love. Stop running. I'm not chasing you anymore . . . just waiting for you.'

She closed her eyes and felt his lips brush her eyelids before they settled, butterfly-light, on her mouth. He deepened the kiss very gradually, making it lovely for her, so that her lips parted without her volition, and even then he didn't take full advantage of her vulnerability, but went on making it sweet, softly exploring her mouth with great tenderness.

Almost, he chased the anger away; she could feel it melting under the impact of this lingering gentleness. But when he drew away she saw the light of triumph in his eyes, in his smile, and the anger came back, hardened again.

He might have seen something in her face, because the smile faded, and his eyes became guarded. He looked at her in silence for some seconds, his expression brooding, thoughtful. Finally he said, 'I'll be in touch, Claire.'

He had thought she would rebuff him if he suggested a date, she knew. He opened his door and when he came round to hers she climbed out of the car in silence, thanked him for the ride and went inside without a backward glance.

When he did contact her again it was by phone. He asked her to go to a dinner-dance with him, a fund-raising function for the hurricane-relief fund. 'Helping out your old friends on the island,' he said. 'I want you to be my partner. We can send them a picture. They'll be thrilled.'

She knew he expected her to refuse, and for a moment she almost did, forgetting her resolution to stop running away and face whatever she had to face squarely. When she accepted there was a short silence before he said, 'Okay. Fine. I'll pick you up that night at seven.'

She wondered if he had had someone else lined up in the event of her refusal. Several someones, probably. Stop that, she told herself. It was futile and pointless. And anyway, he wasn't taking someone else, he was taking her.

She dressed as dazzlingly as she knew how, not so much to impress Scott as to lift her own spirits. It was like putting on armour, she thought as she carefully applied eye shadow to go with the soft, romantic blue of the filmy dress she had chosen and slipped her feet into silver sandals.

He didn't comment on her appearance, but his eyes when he turned and saw her coming into the lounge where he was having a drink with Pietro sparked into quick desire, his face going taut. Inwardly she trembled, but she managed a cool smile as she said, 'I'm not late, am I? Ready?'

He put down his drink without taking his eyes off her and moved to her side. 'Whenever you are,' he said, looking directly into her eyes, watching her pupils widen under his scrutiny. 'Good night, Pietro,' he added over his shoulder. 'Thanks for the drink.'

'Remember . . . she's my daughter,' Pietro said, the friendly tone of his voice almost disguising the warning that lay beneath.

Scott half-turned with his hand resting lightly on Claire's waist. 'I won't forget.'

For a moment the two men eyed each other across the room. Then Pietro nodded. 'Have a good time.'

The dinner was a sumptuous feast of island food, with pork and pineapple and bananas figuring largely, and every second dish swimming in coconut milk. Hibiscus blooms decorated the tables, and the waitresses were garbed in sarongs and grass skirts. Watching her face as she picked a decorative cherry off the top of her coconut-cream dessert, Scott said quietly, 'It's phony as hell, of course, but it's a good way of raising money. Painless for those at this end, and profitable for those on the receiving end.'

'It just seems rather silly,' she said. 'What sort of money has it cost to do this? Couldn't it just have been donated outright?'

'Yes, but committees don't run that way. I'm working on it, though.'

She looked at him. 'You are?'

'Sure. I don't like this, either. I'm here because I'm committee chairman, and the majority voted for this. They said it was a good method of raising funds, and they were right. We stand to make a bomb out of this nonsense. It works. So how can I complain? But I hope we can eventually educate people to give without having to get something for it.'

'I suppose . . .' she said slowly, 'all these people could be spending their Saturday night lining some businessman's pocket while they eat and drink and dance. They might as well enjoy themselves and give to a good cause at the same time.'

'That's the idea. Are you going to eat that, or are you just playing with it?'

'I don't really want it,' she confessed, 'but I don't like to waste it, either.'

'Come and dance,' he suggested, 'and try again later. It's a cold dish. It'll keep.'

They danced, and later danced again, and as the evening wore on, the music, the soft lights, the dancing, began to engender a trancelike state in her. When the music became slow and dreamy she let Scott fold her into his arms and hold her against him, her head drooping on his shoulder, her eyes closed in a kind of lethargic ecstasy. When they sat down he kept his arm about her, his fingers caressing her arm, and she didn't object. Once or twice she thought he looked at her with faint surprise, but they talked little, only touching, moving closely together on the dance floor, their hands entwined, or his arms about her waist and her fingers linked at his neck. She felt the tension slowly building until the evening ended and the cool air hit them as they walked to his car.

He put his hand on the ignition and turned to her. 'Come to my place,' he said. And again she knew she surprised him when she said, 'Yes. All right.'

He hesitated, looked at her again, and then turned the key, bringing the engine to life.

She had never seen his flat. It was not overtly luxurious at all, but comfortable. He had one large painting of a grove of eucalyptus in a wide outback landscape hanging on a plain beige wall, and the oatmeal tweed upholstered sofas were dressed with cushions in chocolate, emerald and gold. It was all understated and casual and very spare.

'You don't like it?' he asked, watching her face.

'Yes, I do. It's just . . . rather unexpected.'

'What did you expect, purple couches and mirrors on the ceiling? I keep those in the bedroom.'

She didn't answer, didn't look at him, and he said, 'Sorry. Have a look round if you like. I'll make coffee.'

She found the bedroom, and it was furnished in gold and deep green, the double bed covered with a heavy-textured woven wool spread. The only mirror was over the long mahogany dressing table. The bathroom was next door, and the fittings were onyx and cream marble. Everything looked very masculine and very tidy.

'Do you do your own housekeeping?' she asked, going back into the lounge as he brought the coffee and placed the two mugs on a table in front of one of the sofas.

'I make the bed and cook. A woman comes three times a week to do the rest.'

She sat down and took up a mug. He came down beside her, close, but not touching her.

'It's all very nice,' she murmured, and sipped. 'You make good coffee, too.'

'Thanks.' He sat back, apparently relaxed, drinking his coffee. But she knew that he wasn't relaxed. He was as tense as she was.

He put his cup down when he had emptied it, but she sat cradling hers, even though there was no coffee left.

'More?' he said, gently removing it from her grasp.

She shook her head. Very deliberately he put the cup beside his own on the table, then turned to face her, his arm on the back of the sofa, his thigh just pressing against her knee. 'I'm wondering why you're here,' he said.

Claire's lips parted, and closed again. She shrugged slightly. 'I'm here because you asked me to come.'

'That's no answer . . . is it? Are you trying to test my willpower . . . knowing I've given my word to Pietro?'

She shook her head vehemently and got up, walking away from him, finding a blind at the window which she raised to look out at a cityscape of lights with the high arch of the Harbour Bridge in the distance.

'I wish I could believe it's because you've changed your mind about marrying me,' he said, 'but I don't think, somehow, that you have, in spite of the way you let me hold you when we were dancing. I can still feel that barrier of barbed wire you've put between us. Why do I get the feeling that you're setting me up for something, Claire? Are you planning some kind of revenge?'

'Why do you want to marry me?' she asked him, suddenly turning to face him.

He rose from the sofa and came over to her, stopping a few feet away. 'Why do you have to ask me that?' he said.

She saw suddenly the anguish in his eyes, and the hope, and the love that had always been hidden from her by his passion.

She wasn't sure when it had happened, but somewhere along the line he had learned to love her. Somewhere he had changed from a man who was intrigued by something unattainable and set himself out to have it, regardless of the consequences, to a man who loved a woman for herself, loved her and wanted to marry her, to live with her for the rest of his life. And she was the woman.

Or perhaps the change was in her mind, in her way of looking at him, seeing him. He had taken her lightly, she had thought, and would forget her in no time, passing on to some new and equally unimportant conquest. Now he was telling her that he had not done that, that what they had shared that night on the island was something that had affected his life, something that mattered to him.

'You love me,' she said, stating a fact.

'Yes,' he answered simply.

'I . . . didn't know.'

He smiled crookedly at her. 'You do now. What are you going to do about it?'

Something seemed to stick in her throat. 'I don't know what to do!' she cried. 'I thought I could marry you, if you didn't love me. . . . It might have been all right, if you only wanted . . . just to make love to me. If it was only passion . . .'

'You're not making any sense. . . .'

'Yes I am! You don't understand.'

'Too right I don't.' His face hardened into a frown. 'So tell me what you're talking about, why don't you?'

'I can't marry you,' she said frantically. 'I can't.'

His face was taut now. 'Because I love you?' he said. 'Or because you don't love me? I don't care. I'll have you on any terms. And after the way you kissed me last time . . . I've had that to hold on to, anyway. . . . you can't tell me you don't feel anything for me.'

'No,' she said. 'I feel too much!'

'Too much of what?' he said carefully. 'Love? Hate?'

Tears suddenly filled her eyes. 'Don't!' she choked. 'Don't. Just take me home. I'm sorry. I shouldn't have come.'

'But you did come, and I'm not taking you home,' he said forcefully. 'Come on, Claire. . . . Tell me what you feel for me. Which is it? Love or hate?'

She shook her head, blindly trying to dispel the tears. 'Both,' she said in a harsh whisper. 'Oh, can't you see? I could hurt you so much!'

'Do you want to hurt me?'

She turned away, lifting her hand to her eyes, angrily dashing away the tears.

He caught her arm. 'Do you?'

'Yes!' she cried fiercely. 'Yes, yes, yes! And I hate myself for it, and I hate you!'

'Well, okay,' he said softly. 'Go ahead. Hit me. You've been wanting to for long enough, haven't you? Do it.'

She stood there shaking, stepping back from him as he came closer until she was against the wall, his eyes pinning her there, angry, wary, daring her.

'You want an excuse?' he said, and reached for her, pulling her into his arms roughly, kissing her mouth with a casual violence that was deliberately insulting. He ground his body against hers in a parody of lovemaking, trapping her against the wall, and then she felt his hands on her breasts, hard and invasive and humiliating.

He let her go and stepped back suddenly, and her hand automatically swung back, her whole being consumed with outrage.

It swung back, and her fingers curled into a fist, and then she saw him standing there before her, waiting, his face flushed but his eyes steady, his mouth tight and hard. Waiting for the blow.

He said, 'Go on.'

And she brought her fist up to her own mouth so hard that her lip stung with the impact, and sobbed, 'No! No. I can't.'

Her fingers spread across her bruised mouth, and she would have collapsed against the wall, only he caught her up in his arms and carried her over to the sofa and cradled her as she went on crying against his shoulder.

'You little fool,' he said, his thumb tentatively exploring her swollen lips. 'What did you do that for?'

'I didn't mean to,' she sighed at last, the tears still falling down her cheeks. 'I didn't mean to.'

He kissed her softly, very gently, and said, 'I'm sorry. I had to get through to you somehow. I couldn't bear you standing there, hating me. I wanted you to get it out of your system.'

She wiped away the last of the tears with the back of her hand and said, 'I'm so tired. I don't think there's any hatred left in me. Take me home.'

He looked down at her drooping eyelids and said, 'No, you can sleep here. I'll phone to tell Pietro that you're staying . . . and that I'll be sleeping on the sofa.'

'He won't like it,' she warned sleepily.

'Too bad. I'll also tell him you're marrying me.'

'I haven't said yes.'

'You're too tired to say anything at the moment. Come on, I'm putting you to bed.'

He did, stripping off her dress and sandals and placing the covers over her, kissing her cheek before he left the room. Vaguely she heard him lift the receiver in the other room; then she sighed and went to sleep.

She woke slowly, convinced that she was dreaming. The sunlight shafted against her closed eyelids, but the slow, delicious stroking of her bare arm and shoulder that had been part of her dream went on. In the dream she had been back on the island with Scott, but it had been broad daylight, and the two of them had swum together and then lain down on the sand, where she had closed her eyes and Scott had begun to touch her quietly, gently, kissing her throat and her shoulder, his fingers drifting over her arms. He was kissing her now, his mouth warm on her shoulder, then just below her ear, then at her nape.

She opened her eyes and said, 'Oh,' and heard his quiet laugh behind her. He turned her to face him, and she saw that he was fully dressed and lying on top of the blankets which covered her.

'You look gorgeous in the morning,' he said, and kissed her mouth, a long, lingering kiss that seemed to last forever. 'Gorgeous,' he said again, resting his head briefly against her breasts. 'I want to look at you.'

She let him fold back the blankets and only stopped him when they slid below her waist.

'Prude!' he said, smiling at her. Then his face changed, softened, and he touched her cheek with his hand. 'Okay, don't look so apprehensive. I promise I'm only looking today. Well, maybe . . .' He dropped his head and put his mouth to her breasts, watching with delight the reaction he had provoked. He put his hands on her then, and bent to her mouth. 'You're going to say yes,' he whispered, 'if we stay here all day. You want to; you know you do.'

'Yes,' she said, closing her eyes, her mouth parting to his kiss. 'Yes.'

He took his time over the kiss, deliberately restrained, although his hands were playing havoc with her senses. 'You did say you'd marry me?' he murmured, breathing in the perfume of her skin.

'I did.'

'Still hating me?'

'No.' She turned her head to kiss his cheek. 'I thought I did. I thought you'd made everything go wrong for me. I wasn't thinking straight. Mother Josephine tried to tell me . . . to get me to admit that it was really myself I was angry with. I just couldn't forgive myself, and I wanted awfully badly to take it out on someone . . . preferably you.'

'Have you forgiven yourself now?'

'I think so. I feel . . . at peace now. Mother Josephine was right. And you were right. Being a nun was an escape for me, from the risk of being hurt again, the risks of loving. There are risks, terrible risks, in loving you.'

'What do you mean?'

'We don't think the same way about things. We don't even share a belief in God, and that's important to me.'

'I know. I won't try to take that from you. I wish I could share it with you. I'd like to believe in someone caring about us all.'

She smiled. 'That's a start.'

'What else?'

'Well, to me marriage is a lifelong commitment . . . a sacrament, something you can't break.'

'That's how I want it to be,' he said.

'*Now* you do.'

'Always. I want our wedding to be in your church, where they believe in that, in always. I want us to be together forever.'

She looked at him and saw that he meant it. 'It's going to be like that,' she said. 'For both of us.'

Gradually he moved away from her and stood up. 'Okay,' he said. 'In that case, I can wait. But please make it soon, my darling, because patience is not my strong suit.'

'I know.'

'I don't want you going through any guilty hang-ups again.'

'You're still not sorry, are you?'

'No,' he said. 'Only for your sake. Because it was traumatic for you, and I just wanted it to be beautiful.'

She put out her hands to him. 'It was,' she said softly. 'It will always be beautiful. Always.'

Silhouette Special Edition

Available Now

A Hard Bargain by Carole Halston

Adam Craddock desperately wanted to buy a valuable piece of
Alabama beachfront. And once he met the owner Whitney
Baines, he knew he wanted her every bit as much!

Winter Of Love by Tracy Sinclair

Even though Shannon and Deke's marriage had dissolved in
divorce, their love never did. And through their son Michael
they would be brought together again, this time, forever.

Above The Moon by Antonia Saxon

When the sky fell in on their perfect world, Kay and Alan were
devastated. But out of their sadness came the strength to build
a new life, with love that would last forever.

Dream Feast by Fran Bergen

Glenn Reeves was a developer who wanted to build a dream.
El Paseo was a part of that dream, but only the owner
Janet Howe, could make his dream complete.

When Morning Comes by Laurey Bright

Claire Wyndham saw Scott Carver as a playboy, a reckless
traveler of the world, a despoiler of hearts—her own included.
Now that he'd taken her heart, should she give him
her soul, also?

The Courting Game by Kate Meriwether

It would have been a routine case if Courtney Ross' adversary
had been anyone except millionaire Blaz Devlin.
In his embrace she realized she might lose the case,
and her heart, as well.